THE
DEEP NORTH

Also by Fanny Howe

Poetry

Eggs
The Amerindian Coastline Poem
Poem from a Single Pallet
Alsace Lorraine
For Erato: The Meaning of Life
Introduction to the World
Robeson Street
The Lives of a Spirit

Prose

Forty Whacks
First Marriage
Bronte Wilde
Holy Smoke
The White Slave
In the Middle of Nowhere

THE
DEEP
NORTH

FANNY HOWE

Sun & Moon Press
Los Angeles, California

© Fanny Howe, 1988
Cover: Colleen McCallion
Design: Katie Messborn

Library of Congress Cataloging-in-Publication-Data

Howe, Fanny
  The Deep North / Fanny Howe

    p. cm. ⌐ (New American Fiction Series: 15)
  ISBN: 1-557-13025-6: $12.95
  ISBN: 1-557-13026-4: $30.00 (signed cloth)
    I. Title. II. Series
  PS3558.089D44 1988   88-24896   CIP
  813' .54—dc 19
  New American Fiction Series: 15

---

10 9 8 7 6 5 4 3 2 1

Published by
Sun & Moon Press
6148 Wilshire Boulevard
Gertrude Stein Plaza
Los Angeles, California 90048

THE
DEEP NORTH

At first it wasn't clear. No truth. No belongings. There was snow on the trees, rooftops, streets and that gray light you see in old movies set at sea, where ice floes break the boat apart. This to me is the image of the knowable. Ropes and stripes, black and white, and what you look at, looks back. If it's a dream, or if it's what is actually seen, then it comes to the same thing: broken language, foreign syntax, the incomprehensible nature of the world.

Anyway I didn't even want an answer, that's a fact. All answers are hells. I just wanted to locate the process that underlay the surface image, to put my hand under the top without looking at what I let out. Whatever it was, it didn't belong to me.

One night two small children roamed the woods alone. Their mother, who was fondling some man, and their father, who was self-absorbed, didn't notice. A highway of moonlight cut through the spruce and scrub of the Cape woods and they heard the distant crush of waves on sand. No one, for that time, really cared where they were. The effect of alcohol, which children learn to dread, made them fly into the warm night air. Their pajamas damp around the hems, they trotted hand in hand, into the thickets, silent of birdsong, though fog horn called *forlorn* to fog horn.

The boy was the guide. The girl let him lead her because he was four years older. Pretend, he said, we are slaves escaping. You're the slave and I'm the master's son. You said I want to go to the North with you, so I took you with me late one night. You were actually the illegitimate daughter of the master, too, by a slave woman who had very pale skin. I was incredibly brave, so I agreed to take you, like this, to the river where a canoe would meet us. Okay?

His story raced down tne tracklines laid by the moonshine and trees and watercolor shadows danced on the gray trunks, as they passed. Her eyes were teary with excitement, it was so late, and her real parents so far behind. Her conviction that they would notice she was gone, and get mad, made her stomach stir round and round, and she held tight to her brother's hand, so the lines on their palms pressed.

When we get to the end of the river, the boy continued, we will be met by a party of escaped slaves and Indians. I will leave you with them, and they will raise you in the wilderness, as one of them, while I roam the country, alone. . . .

That night they lay on the sand dunes huddled in a knot. She was unable to sleep for thinking about her freedom and staring at the night sky and its illuminating stars. Only the black sky, with the sea smoking nearby, could inform her of her position as God's agent on earth. Her brother was twelve, she was eight. She was sure this escape was connected to her proximity to a Divine Being, even though she lived in a family of committed atheists. The weight of her little head on her brother's arm numbed him to sleep while her eyes gained access to those showers of stars. At last she was free from the blank eyes of her mother, and her father's vocal competence. As her brother's little sister in American history, she felt she was also freed of a future where grown-ups never changed. That intransigence, when finally believed and accepted, was more horrible than the thought of eternity. Like the appetite of the ocean, going back and forth and nowhere special, it was character itself.

In the dark the water seemed to pour out of the sky, and at dusk it came in gray, a form of air denser and wetter by weight alone. At the murky horizon, she saw how the water poured from space. But what, then, were the red rose balls, the nettles, the clover, lace and goldenrod, the spruce and shrubbery which together murmured as if a spirit was locked inside? A little boxweed smell filled the dewy air. Crows quarreled and small birds sang. Gulls bit at the tops of the caving water, white to white.

When she finally slept, the boy woke up to watch and listen to the sun unveiling the world. Landscape is all that greets the most enormous desires, even if only the landscape of a face. He looked at his sister's untroubled sleep, placid and closed like a law, and seeing that she was no longer a brown-skinned and brave slave, but the familiar sister he saw at home, he pulled away his arm and ran back up the beach on his own.

One August day the mother, father and daughter were driving together through Boston. They were going to visit the brother where he was bedded in a single hospital room. He was six- teen and suffering from asthma. They were running tests on him to find out if he might have an allergy to something at home, which he said he did.

It was 1952. The daughter, G, had returned from summer camp, brown from sun, her black hair streaked gold and still, in her camp clothes, she smelled of pine and oil. The vacancy of her green-eyed stare—she was now twelve—expressed the shock in visual juxtaposition between this hot and steamy street and the valleyed green of Vermont.

Her parents were quiet, which was not normal. Usually, if one was quiet, the other was not. The mother's classy New York accent gave to her voice a complacent tone, which the father, a New Englander, had absorbed and integrated into his own nasal twang. This influence of her on him was perhaps the only one any outsider might notice.

G wanted them to talk, as if their words, like shells tossed up from the ocean, were reassuringly refined and enduring. Look, she said, Look at that man!

He was lying on the curb, his face pressed into the concrete, red and scraped.

If you look closely, Dear, the mother responded, you'll see he's lying outside a bar. That means he's drunk, nothing to worry about.

They stopped at a set of lights, and she could see almost the length of the street running under the el to Forest Hills station. As a place that never sees light, it looked like the inside of an unhappy life. Its density of object and shadow, of billboards, neon, trash and dark-skinned humanity, put a reflection into G's eyes, like reminiscence transplanted into the present. "An added look," as they say. Her parents began talking when the light changed. The mother started:

I don't care what Dr. Simon says. Tonio was born high-strung.
Asthma at this age? No. He's putting on an act.
    Well, it may be an act and it may not be. But Dr. Simon is in
charge now, and we have to take him seriously. He says it's
asthma.
He says it's asthma, Tonio says it's an allergy. I say it's nerves.
    Maybe it's all three, the father suggested.

The mother then sighed high in her throat, almost a hiss. G
heard these sighs of her mother's as the background music to
her own emotions and experiences, as if her mother's voice
was her private soundtrack. She sighed herself, a minimal
puff, and her stomach made a motion on its own. She was
often afraid of each member of her family, though she had no
idea why.

She knew her brother was up to something; he didn't want to
come home unless it was conditional. On what, she couldn't
guess. G always felt, within feet of her brother, a change in the
air's content. A tunnel has a similar effect, especially when
you have to turn on the headlights entering it from daylight.

Remembering his black hair and olive skin, his green eyes and wide red mouth—a composition not unlike her own features, but paler and more aquiline—she put him, now, in some lofty frame. His moods, which frightened her at home, now seemed connected to the streets around, their aura of tragedy and injustice.

Outside, the air was wobbling around hot traffic and people, while the car circled a concrete grid supporting the el. The heat made watery ribbons across the surfaces of things, as if it lived inside those things and didn't ignite from above. G leaned out her window to watch the activity, to smell the airs and hear the voices. Inside she contained the traces of that black lake water with its iron qualities, its reflections of pine and stone; but she pulled herself away voluntarily. She wanted to know where her brother was placed, and was reassured by the way the people outside were taking the heated streets for granted.

How can people live like that, said the mother with a trace
of disgust.
Dunno, he replied and went on to speculate about lowered
expectations among the poor. I think they just get used to it,
he concluded. Besides, this isn't real poverty. They should go
to India to see what real poverty is.

The hospital was down a small side street, empty of activity.
    Is this the way you came when you brought him? G asked.
Yes . . . Now Anna, you take Gemma and go on in. I'll park.

This was the way they usually did it. The mother was left at
the door while the father parked, even if only a few feet away.
Now A, small and tanned, approached the entrance to the
hospital as if it were her possession. This was always her way
of dealing with the world. In her late forties, she was buoyant,
thirtyish and vain. Her face was straight-lined in structure, except for a small indentation in her chin. She had the green
eyes, brownish complexion and black hair of her children because of her Italian mother—an "aristocrat," according to A.

Now G, in the wake of the mother's perfume, drifted after her,
to the elevator. The familiar click-click of the high heels ahead
of her made her believe, for a spell, that the world was com-
posed of efficiencies.

Hey, called the father, rushing up behind them. Here I am.
    So you are!
The two of them drew together automatically, the image of
lucky-in-love and lucky-in-money, though not, at a glance,
suited to each other. His small sandy features—mouth and
chin measured in trim proportions—were those of a thoughtful, well-bred boy. Pleasures of youth were preserved by his
loosened tie, scuffed shoes, and frayed seersucker jacket, but
his brow was furrowed, as if to remind the world that he was in
fact thoughtful and grown-up. His hair, worn in an overlong
crewcut, spiked a couple of inches above his skull, and his lips
were frequently pursed. He had a habit of pulling his horn-
rimmed glasses up and down the length of his nose, suggesting that the world was a book and he was constantly dipping
into it.
    Tonio is expecting us, isn't he, asked G.
Of course he is, the father said, and he put his hand on G's
shoulder, steering her into the elevator. (She wore, by the way,
a look of terror which she hoped someone would notice; they
didn't.)

They found T in his bed, under the covers. The sun lay heavy
on the thin white sheets. He was curled up, his eyes shut with
his long black lashes deepening the blue shadows under the
lids. G, seeing him so reduced, looked away and blushed.

Darling, said his mother.

He lurched upright, all in one move, then stayed on his elbows, propped up and frowning.

Why did you bring Gemma here?

She wanted to see you. She's just back from camp.

It was not a physical family. No kisses accompanied this explanation. Instead G stepped back and looked around the
room for something she might like. Leaf shadows danced on a
white wall; she slipped to the window to find their source.

How are you today, Dear? Sleepy? What's the doctor saying to you about coming home?

Nothing.

It's bound to be soon. Tomorrow maybe? the father noted.

I hope not. . . . If I do, I'll just get sick again. Besides, the two of you do just fine without me there.

No, we don't. Don't be silly.
Oh Mother, don't lie.

Mother? You mean "Mummy," she corrected him.
Did you learn any songs at camp, Gemma? the father suddenly asked. This was a familiar signal and G whirled around from the window, obediently. Her face was rounder for his question and her eyes brighter.

Do I have to? she inquired.
The father nodded and smiled at the other members of his family, as if to say that at last he had found the key to their happiness. G opened her mouth and closed her eyes and sang in a high but strong voice. She was trying not to giggle, and clutched her hands in fists.

"By the Green Mountain water
With the moon in the trees
I laid down my rug and paddle
And knew I was free.
    Yodel-ay-whoo-whoo!
    Yodel-ay-hay-hay!
    I was free!"

Are you going to Italy? the boy asked his parents. His interruption was his judgement on his sister's performance.
I don't think so, said the mother.
    Too bad. I hoped you'd all be away for a while.
Well, sorry to disappoint you, said the father who had often expressed his conviction that T was spoiled and not nervous, or sick, ever. It was obvious to everyone in the room that he was now about to say just that, because he looked down at his son with his lips locked into a dangerous knot, and his glasses up across his eyes for a hard reading.

G stared out the window, but her face was blazing. She heard her brother's voice crack as he began to react.
    Gemma, take yourself for a walk down the hall, said the
    father in a falsely good-humored tone.
Hurriedly, the girl did as she was told and walked the hall the way they had come. Her hands were gluey and her stomach churned. The smells she brushed against made her feel ill, and she was torn between the desire to stare at the patients and to pretend they didn't exist. Wasn't disease catching; so why put all the sick people near each other where they'd get sicker? She stared at the floor, and gasped a quick breath, stopped at the elevator, held her nose and guided her shadow back again.

Then she stood outside the door to T's room, listening. A nurse was in there now. She had an accent and a voice that reminded G of the smell of vanilla.

You don't want to get him upset now, she was saying to the parents. That can set off another attack, you know.

He's faking, the mother was saying. Believe me. I know him.

I don't think you can fake an asthma attack, the nurse replied.

You'd be surprised, said the mother. It's time for him to come home.

I don't want to go home, Mother, said T.

But why not?

I'm allergic to it.

Oh come on. That's so childish. You're just like my mother's family—high strung. It comes with the breeding. But in this country it's too hard to survive with that kind of sensibility. That's what's wrong with you. Inherited sensitivity—

You two are acting like idiots, said the father. Fight, fight, fight is all you ever do. Now what are you after, Tonio? Just say what you want and let's get on with it.

If I go home, I want my freedom. That's all. Not much. Freedom?

Yes. I'm suffocating. That's the meaning of asthma. I don't even have a car.

A car? Is that what you want? asked the mother. Then she said to the nurse, as if to a maid: You can leave now.

And now the nurse walked by G, shaking her head the way people do all over the world. She was as brown as a bottle of vanilla, and G wanted to follow her, but didn't dare leave the door.

By the way, Pa, she heard T say in a loud voice. Speaking of meaning. What's the meaning of life?

Dunno. But when you figure it out, don't tell me.

Now his family left T; they used the stairs this time, in single file and speechless. When they stepped out onto the street, they were met by the bright hot sun, and it was as shocking as if they had been inside at a midday movie. The father looked perplexed, as he often did, while the mother caressed her upper arms with her fingers. Inside the car no one spoke, but passing back again under the rattling tracks of the el, G stared into the slums of Boston and perceived them as a form of x-ray, a study of the inside of the self, which she could not interpret.

In a matter of hours, her brother was released from there, never to return. In the months to come, with a car at his disposal, he was hardly ever home; he was off in the mountains, skiing, when he wasn't at school. The mysterious attack of asthma never recurred.

At the end of one August, when G was small, a woman was hired by the family to be their maid. Her name was Darlene; she was originally from the deep South. She was a petite, pretty woman with coffee-colored skin and a long neck. She seemed to see speech rather than to hear it. Her eyes flew up and down and around catching the words, then let them settle, before she would respond with an expression of intense visual focus on her face. She read voraciously in hours snatched between cooking and cleaning. She read the Russian novelists, and books on European and American history, and sometimes she was annoyed with G for hanging around. She called G "the dark little white girl" and so did Ron, her fiance, whom she had followed to Boston. G often sat in the kitchen after school and talked alone to Darlene or listened to her and Ron speaking across the table, stove, sink. G sometimes sat on top of the refrigerator with her legs hanging over the pictures she had drawn, which her father had hung there. She watched Darlene read in the same tidy way she did everything else. She sat erect on the edge of the kitchen chair and turned the pages slowly, pensively, occasionally gazing off into space.

As she grew older G was aware that her parents' world was in turmoil over issues related to Russia and Communism. At dinner these were the topics. Names like Welch, McCarthy, Hiss and Chambers were like titles of books on espionage. The names were code-words in war and conjured up images of tall grass, safaris, guns and gas. The adult world was a system of concealment and hidden decisions, tremendous ambition and attention to surface. G's father was an administrator in an arts and scholarship foundation. Feeling himself to be on the side of the enemy (money), he went out of his way to stay close to professors and artists and to sustain a political position that would allow him to live twice: once as a manager of time and money, second as a thinker and liberal. It was a difficult balance. As if he had two eyes looking in separate directions, he was often heard to say, "I see what you mean, but on the other hand. . . ."

The family lived in a wooden frame house on a rural street. Crabapple and Japanese cherry trees, bleeding hearts, tiger lilies, lily of the valley, violets, myrtle and wild columbine lathered the garden as well as the August and autumn flowers, orange and red like the leaves. The mother raised a little vegetable garden in boxes; beans and peas climbed up strings. Inside the house the wallpaper was flowered. The downstairs rooms were furnished by the eighteenth-century Europeans; but the rugs were Persian. These rooms sat in a eerily expectant state like stage sets.

There was an upright piano in the study, and this was for G to play while her father read at his desk. He had insisted that she have lessons in music, singing, dancing, and he hung her drawings all over the house. He called her his girl wonder and liked to have her perform for him and others, though she squirmed, writhed and hated it. When he watched her singing, or dancing, his eyes acquired a dreamy expression, his tense features softened and his became the face he was gazing on. He saw a great future for her, and participated in its planning as if she were a little spirit he had unleashed from inside himself and he could steer it forward, a part of himself, into a victorious future. His own sense of failure was prodigious.

While the father reveled in G's accomplishments and always begged for more, he never seemed to see her in the hours between them. So she was surprised, and even hesitant, when he took her for a walk in the woods soon after T returned home from the hospital. He told her what the names of trees were (a maple he identified as an elm and a birch as a beech) and kept his hand on the back of her neck which she held rigid. He told her how she was like his side of the family and he said that he and she shared a certain view of the world which would always help them understand each other. She was proud to the point of blushing and her mind filed through ways to please him. But something, at the same time, held her tongue. She was afraid, she realized, to say or do anything clever because he would at once forget her and make an event out of the act. He would make her take lessons if she sang in the car, or doodled while she talked on the phone, or if she told him she could identify a scarlet tanager. So now she didn't dare do anything at all but walk stiffly by his side, inhaling his attentions.

His hand played at the nape of her neck, his thumb trailing in and out of the soft groove there, and they gazed into the varying depths of shadow and light, greens so hard they were nearly black, and he told her what she was and who she was and where she would be in twenty years, till the sun was like a spill of liquid, ferns were like ironed Christmas trees and mushrooms were like penises, and nothing was exactly what it was, but like something else. She smelled skunk cabbage and its odor clung inside her nostrils, merging with her feelings about herself. She scooted, then, out from inside his hand and went to tug up a stalk of grass to wear between her teeth. It arced out in front of her as she walked an arm's length away from him. She saw from the corner of her eye that his hand was still raised to receive the back of her neck again, but she pretended she didn't see, until it went down.

A white bird leaves the snow.
Gradual disentanglement from cars and chickenish seagulls.
Watch my monkey-tricks now, I'm unearthly too—without
cream toner, moisturizer shampoo or conditioner; but my will
does not belong to the I who is directing it.
Madness is a loss of moral sense. You know this when you
have a mad person in the house and wonder where their brain
screws into the divine scheme.

Nobody knows where I've been—its emergencies, its gusti-
ness, its huddled beggary in welfare offices—no one knows
the people in trouble I've been and seen. Fists racing at my
face, stacked in an alcove where I escaped into politics and
bottles. No one but those who are there all the time have seen
the underworld close up in this town.
Where flashlights are like watch-fires, the torsos are removed
from incinerators and elevator shafts. In this city of low forms,
my anguish is an echo, the story of a story. That's not good
enough when your desire is too big for your body. The American experiment has shattered in the lab.

Many years later, on a train to New York, G forgot who she was. She was gazing out the window at apartment buildings—some hammered shut and some occupied—against a floral pink sky. She had a pair of seats to herself and she rocked uneasily with the motion of the train. Her hands were folded on her lap, her left still wearing the garnet engagement ring and gold band of her early marriage. The train, then, entered the tunnel approaching Penn Station. As if she were turning to gold, a numbness came down her skull, moved through her neck, shoulders, chest, arms and on, all the way to her feet until she was a shell with not even the hiss of the wind inside.

The experience, as she knew at the time, was called a massive anxiety attack. The name didn't produce relief, but its opposite. The terror increased. Like desire going backwards, and backwards, obliterating all hope and imagination. G, then, for the first time ever, forgot her name, where she was coming from and where she was going, and viewed herself as an alien among aliens, a particle supported only by the density of an indifferent eternity. Around her, people were getting restless, pulling down their bags, putting on their coats. She didn't move, even when someone dropped down close beside her. It was a woman darker than herself, with an overnight bag on her knees.

G was black-haired, green-eyed, and browntoned like her mother, but her feelings about this likeness disgusted her. Sitting in the train that day, doused in sweat, she tried to restore herself by turning to the woman beside her. That placid dark face she read as a sign of kindness and wisdom.

I'm sick of traveling. It makes me feel sick, she said.

That's too bad, was the low reply.

Do you like to travel?

I don't know. I just do it.

Are you from Boston?

The woman did not answer but tipped out to the side and looked down the aisle as if she had suddenly remembered a runaway child. G ran her wet hand across her wet brow. Then she pulled her sketchbook out of her bag and flipped it open to a page where she had drawn pictures of old men in a park. Black webbed lines, spidery, incomplete. Her father would have loved them.

The woman glanced at the picture and asked, Why did you make those people so ugly? That's unkind.

Ugly?

Look at his nose.

It's an exaggeration.

Hm. Not in my eyes.

G closed the sketchbook back in her bag. She said aloud but to herself, I have to take the world as it is. I have to accept reality. I have no choice. The woman looked at her knowingly, then rose to her feet and departed down the aisle.

The train lurched, stopped and the platform was dim but deserted outside the window. G, glancing at her own face mirrored over that image, was taken aback by the glitter of her eyes and the ferocity of her own expression. She wondered, aimlessly, who she was and where she was going. Someone so fierce should know these facts. The figures swimming beyond her face were like reflections in a deep pond, a trail of souls moving through murky light, everybody lost.

She hauled out her bag from under her seat and headed outside, knowing she would take the first train back the way she came. Anxiety ("depression," her mother would say) curled back inside her like a creature that fears the motion of its nest, her body. It went in, and as it did, more than the mere statistics of her person returned. As she climbed the stairs with the crowd, her eyes fixed on the concrete floor, she remembered pleasure, as hard and for as long as she could.

She had hoped to leave her husband, Adam, and to make a
new life in New York. The way they talked to each other was
frightening to her—he in the language of Freud, of Wilhelm
Reich, of others who saw the psychological subject as being
the whole person. This was his field, and he was young in it
and couldn't resist explaining herself to herself in those terms.
"You are functioning with a diminished libido and a fear of
separation bordering on psychosis," he might say. Or: "You
suffer from an enlarged super-ego which dominates the infan-
tile aspects of your personality. This keeps you at a level of
suspended and unfulfilled genital fixation." He told her that
the Civil Rights movement was a misplaced rebellion against
the father on the part of adolescents. If she said she believed
in something, he said she really meant that she was "interested" in that something.

At the same time Adam was hot-blooded and could hardly
get enough of her sexually. This pleasure bound them to
each other long after the mental wounds they inflicted on
each other had become permanent. G had many talents—
dramatic, artistic, musical, scholarly—but they were like dis-
tractions compared to the quest that drove her forward. His
whole-heartedness in his work was the equivalent of this quest
of hers; yet hers, vague and unnamed, was useless in the world.

The military is on standby, not really. Why all this technology then? Rehearsing the murder of the world? Coming events can affect present experience. For instance, I'm approaching someone who doesn't even know it. Unfulfilled volition doesn't die, but lives until its chance comes again.

What's the difference between being alive and being a machine?
The stone feels nothing, not its atoms or time. Metal colors layer the water, leathery leaves cover the ground.
To be fully human is my greatest desire. A system of mystical ethics should follow when I'm killed for it.
An S of benches and prickly fruit trees shows me, as I approach, that my action and my time are one and the same.
Am I moving now toward the future or am I the eye that sees distant blossoms in a huddle of sparrows?

In 1950 the family spent the month of August with their uncle at Lago di Garda in the North of Italy. They had been there once before, right after the war when the first civilian air flights were just back in operation. The plane bumped across the Atlantic while people threw up and had ear aches of epic proportions. The mother was eager to see her uncle with whom she had lost contact for the better part of her youth and marriage. This man, and Italy itself, were territories she considered her own in some deep mythic sense. They freed her to be more than a mere American, in the eyes of other Americans.

The uncle met them at the train. He was a tall balding man, with a big bouquet of flowers for each member of the family and a hired limousine to take them to his mountain home. G was still clutching at her agonized ears, while her brother wore a savage mask of nausea. But none of them was too uncomfortable to notice the landscape and the architecture, spare and pastoral. They passed through light, empty streets and on to the lake, where pink flowers dashed out of the stones and the blue water was painted with mountains. Boats buzzed, and scooters sped by their car, but no machine could undermine the grace of that misty air.

That August the uncle sat in a wicker chair on the lawn, under a straw hat, his silences profound. He gave no indication that he was glad any one of them was visiting.

Don't take it personally, A told her husband and children again and again. He's always been moody.

The children didn't mind his quiet, though G sometimes tried to win him over by doing little acts and skits in front of his chair. In the evenings they ate pastas, salads, fruit, cheeses and breads; then the children would sit and listen to adult conversation which, in this context, contained an urgency and intelligence otherwise missing. There was a lot of war talk, politics, subjects P and A rarely mentioned when alone together, but often in company. P had been in Germany at the end of the war, Britain in the beginning and never in active combat. It was just desk work, he said.

The uncle didn't like to talk much about where he had been, and only gave the most minute details about hiding in the mountains and, finally, in Switzerland. T, who had read a lot about strategy, the Napoleonic wars, torture and Aryan superiority, insisted on interrupting and asking questions. His love of drama made him bloodthirsty and his love of his mother made him want to appear as intelligent as his father. That was hard. P was a man who alternated between bewilderment and authority. He talked at length, aimlessly but eloquently, giving the impression that he knew a great deal about most every subject. Indeed, he often told experts in one field or another all about their subjects. He was known to be exactly wrong on every topic. He almost had the facts, but not quite, and he was so nice, no one ever corrected him. Not even his wife.

While the men talked, on those evenings, she got drunk and roamed through the perfumed gardens, restless and depressed. Her doll-like face became slack and flushed; her eyes looked inward; and all her senses were awash in emotion. T, furiously, watched her through the screening darkness, and when she flung herself over the father's back, twisting her fingers through his belt, T leaped up and retreated with great sighs. G, figuring he knew something she didn't, followed making gagging noises. It was all an act on her part; she was not yet aware of adult sensuality. Her parents didn't interest her nearly as much as T himself did.

That summer his self-interest was total. And G, flashing around the edges of his smudged looking-glass eyes, was about as interesting to him as a passing bird. He lived in books, and emerged with a passion for himself as the reader. By the act of reading, he had made all that happen. War, redemption, romance. He affected a limp and believed he was the replica of Andre in *War and Peace*, learning his speeches by heart. Sometimes he stood with his hand on his breast, like Napoleon, and sometimes he kept his hands in his pockets and looked up from under, moodily, like Leslie Howard in *Gone with the Wind*. G, his enraptured audience, still kept him from going too far.

She developed a series of routines in Italy. Most of them were imitations of T himself—one showed him lying on the grass tossing and gasping and complaining about the terrible heat of the sun and equally terrible chill of swimming; another showed him yawning sequentially and insisting he wasn't tired at all. Then she had one of her mother mincing around on very high heels, and stumbling over the gravel, with her fingers extended as if for drying nails, and asking if someone would please shake her up a martini. G had the hardest time doing an imitation of her father. While she tried acting him out as an absent-minded professor, T called directions at her which contradicted her plan. Then her father himself appeared, and not realizing whom she was imitating, became involved in giving her acting lessons and made her recite "To be or not to be" in a monotone. If she protested, he looked pained, and this action of his later became the one by which she imitated him.

The old uncle had a small yellow airplane with four wings, which he flew twice a week, taking no one with him. He went up alone, and sometimes flew right over the house while the family waved up at him. When he was gone on these excursions, the tempo of the household picked up, and spirits lightened, and each person realized how strong an effect one person's character can have on a group. The mother painted toes and fingers; the father drew from his briefcase a folded copy of the *New York Times* crossword puzzle. It was a sign, always, that he was ready to relax and retreat pleasurably. If you can get the upper left-hand corner of a puzzle, you can get the whole thing, he always said. And indeed he would complete the upper left-hand corner with words and definitions that fit, but were wrong. And then he'd go on to the rest of the puzzle, which became more and more frayed and complex as time went by. Finally he'd stuff the puzzle in a wastebasket and wait for the next Sunday's.

One day the uncle emerged from the house in a leather aviator's jacket and cap, and boots too. The father looked perplexed, as if he was not sure whether a laugh was expected. He got no help from the mother who looked, for once, equally surprised. After all, that outfit was dated by decades and evoked unhappy memories of war. The uncle was not a joker, though. Everyone clung to that one historical fact as he strode past the borders of tall flowers, pink and yellow, to the car. No one even smiled. He turned and said, Go down to the beach and watch me fly.

What fun! Of course we will! cried the mother and got to her feet.

In about an hour, he said sternly and continued his departure.

When he was gone, the parents shrugged and murmured, and T went on and on about the priceless beauty of the leather uniform and how he wished he had one just like it. The father then went into a lengthy explanation about the history of aviation and war, and G stood like a stork, one bare foot lifted to rest on the other knee, staring off into space. The sky that day was whitish blue, with a suffusing silence that seemed to take everything in: buzzes, splashes, whistles, talk.

Later the family trooped down to the lakeside, where dinghies of all colors were laid upside down, and they sat with their feet hanging off the dock, looking nonchalant or cynical. Finally the toy-like buzz of the yellow plane was heard over the mountains, and they watched it emerge from the whiteness. Nobody spoke. The plane, releasing a plume of white smoke, pointed its nose upwards and rose in an arc, directly over the center of the lake. Then the silence took over, like shock; the engine stopped; slowly, gracefully, the plane dropped straight down, turning in circles, the smoke left high up behind. It fell right to the top of the lake, and bounced and sank, while the family watched. It happened very fast. A motorboat shot out across the water to where it fell.

Take Gemma to the house, the father told T.

But what happened, Pa, what happened? the boy asked.

His voice quivered and cracked as it had when it was changing. His sister was crying. He dragged her up the rough, stony lane, between banks of vines and wildflowers with a tender and bitter smell. The two of them looked back and up, stumbling, like those witnesses to an apparition of Mary which appears only to children.

Some vocal intonation testifies as to the word's meaning. I steer my body north, salt in my eyes, humming as the dog leaps the cones of snow. White covers where the spring hides carnations plumper than fluff.

I think sensuality perverted causes pain and elicits a sense of tragedy which is all biological. Blocked love is a torment tighter than a throat. In the context of repressed desire, a blush either means shame or pleasure. I understand the sign of a wagging tail better than a human laugh.

In one Boston bar vodka is forbidden as being too "soviet". I love white wine so my tongue can wash away its daily cursing. Then reflections on a car's windshield make me remember danger and only music circling my head lets me pulse again.

One Saturday G went to the school she hated, a brick building at the crest of a green hill, and she climbed the fire escape, slid up a window she had unbolted the day before, and climbed inside. It was raining outside. She was fourteen when she stood with the curtains twisted in her hands and wrists and looked at her own colorful image on the glass, like the face of a young saint in a church. Then she cracked open a little box of matches and lit the curtains, watched the fire surround her face, and climbed out the window and down the escape, ran and rang the fire alarm in the red box at the side of the street, and walked home, dragging her hot sneakers through puddles.

In 1959, August, G received a letter from T who was in the Army:

> Gemma—I seem to get no farther than your name across the page. An hour ago I sat down in this tent, thinking to write before dark. Now the lantern is lighted and still I have nothing written.
>
> Your letter came today. It was strange. I do not understand the parts about love and happiness, but the solitude I do. Rilke (I think) says of solitude: "Thou art as rich and clean and wide as an awakening garden." Sometimes I think of this, and how solitude is the price of freedom. I know you always wanted freedom more than anything else.
>
> Gemma—your letter is very serious for you. Are you very much in love with this man? I guess you must be. The trouble is, what you say is hard for me to translate where I sit here. I really can't understand my past, our past, or why I'm here, but here I am! The pine needles are still warm from the sun, and wind waves like a sea through the trees and it's cold under my field jacket. My hands smell of oil and canvas, wood smoke and sun. My head is heavy and my jaw rough from shaving in cold water. Under the little writing table, near my feet, are my helmet and pistol belt. Shadows move on the tent walls and soon it will be my turn at guard.

Why I like it, I couldn't tell you. I conjure up enemies—
yellow men, black men—whom I chase through the tall
pines. At night I creep silently, with the other men, bathed
in cool stinking sweat and mud from the swamps and wanting cigarettes so bad, I could scream. We eat mostly out of
tins because fires are illegal on maneuvers. As long as I can
pretend I hate someone out there in the dark, I find I can
turn with love to my fellow soldiers and continue to wage
this hot and bloody mock war. I think a person needs to
invent an enemy if one isn't provided naturally.

Please keep in touch with me. I worry about you and
your attitudes. You must not try to outdo your liberal background with anarchic politics. Just because your environ-
ment is one way, it doesn't mean you have to be another. I
hate to think of you married. And to a Jew! I have to say
that. You're too young and all men are shits.

Save yourself for—

T

I can't live without hope even when my head is aching.

The terrible things I've done to survive! Think—the last seven years of doing what I must, out of duty. Do I get a break, a reward?

When I meet the hatred inculcated in me since childhood, it is discharged in action, a surprise to me.

Everything living into the present has an effect on the future. Unnoticed horizons exist, I think.

I dreamed I was a boy sailing on the sea and at last a man
would lie down and hold me.
Home, I want to leave you. But the move is too long, the
weather too cold for you to take yourself out today or ever.
Fish in an aquarium can't be moved either.

If you don't want prediction, take risks. In this way the small
change of legal thought can often be discovered in a city bed.
Like a boy bathing in a river with electric wires, prediction is
one way to choose the next shock.

During one winter the tremors set off by surrounding politics became more personal than usual. The parents' voices murmured and snapped in dark corners after the lights were lit elsewhere. They disagreed about things going on outside, and even about their own histories. The nut-brown mother walked around with a glass in her hand; she smoked and sat with her skirt raised far above her knee, her eyes bored or yearning. Always dressed in expensive and fashionable clothes, with her curls bobbed around her ears, in a dim light she looked very pretty and young. Habitually she studied her calves, the slope of her ankle down to her foot and her hands, at a distance, and at length. She liked having money and wearing it too.

Money was a political issue. How she handled their checkbook was a major subject of interest. She had inherited all of her uncle's money after his sky suicide, and the house in Italy as well, but P wanted none of it. Uncle Joe had, as it turned out, been a Nazi collaborator during the war and the property in Italy and his acquired wealth were, to P, tainted by this association. But A said, If you had been in Italy during the war, you would have been a collaborator too.

She loved having the Italian house, her own income and the independence they gave her. Where before she had been under P's rule, now she defied and talked back at him.

Like her daughter and Darlene, A also giggled about her husband's friends, but right in front of him. She couldn't, she said, stand either ideas or ideology. For two decades she had a lover, one of P's painter friends, and A was the first, in public, to joke about the man's being "a fairy." Meantime A and he met once a week, every Thursday, in his studio in the Back Bay and joyfully made a joke of the reputation she had begun for him. Since she inherited the house in Italy, she developed a slight Italian accent and wore only the clothes she purchased over there; P drove a battered old Ford to work and fussed about the high cost of educating his children in private schools.

If you don't want any of the Italian money, that's fine with me, A told her husband. I'll keep it for myself while you play poor.

He didn't argue with her, but rubbed his head and made a joke about the high cost of loving.

You old fraud, she teased. You old goose. Do geese see
God? Can you say that backwards?

Do . . . gee . . . see . . . odd, go . . . dog?

Try again! It's a palindrome!

She had learned it from her lover, among other word games
she ran around her bewildered spouse. He had a new style
himself. It was modeled on certain European professors he
admired, and was meant to supply the aging process with dig-
nity. He wore his hair longish, tossed gray to the side, and his
face acquired a melancholy cast, the handsome weakness
there was shrouded now in a sort of fashionable gloom. His
work was completely administrative, but he passed for a great
scholar now with his tweeds and long gray hair.

The premises are now sealed and sold. Tenants gone.
It's on the other side of the tracks I want to be when the snow
spills creamily down a set of stone lips.
I see the halfway girl, whose baby was taken away, balance on
the cushion stuffing. Bags are stacked in the hall, and around
the basement burner.
Damp places hold in the ruin and never the fun.

The boy now a man on a bed is dreaming of fishing. Give him
your net, fisherman of heaven, and multiply the glitter of his
illusions.

In time it must all make sense, the suffering sent forth from
one body into many.

At eighteen G was a Communist sympathizer, who also drank too much—sweetened alcohols of any source or color, and like her mother, she smoked and preened her hands and feet. She was set to graduate from college a year early, and her friends were activists and beatniks with reputations, like hers, based on intellectual brilliance and wild behavior. Her figure was dark and skitterish and her tangled curls and blazing green eyes won her the nickname Haywire-and-Gemstone.

Where are you from? people would ask her. Here, she would say and wince. I'll be leaving soon though, and I won't come back. I hate Boston. It's an anglophile jungle.

Once in a darkened bar, she was giving a detailed account of the class structure in Boston, when she was noticed by her husband-to-be, Adam, where he sat with his friends nearby.

How can they serve her alcohol? She looks fourteen, he said.

Haven't you ever seen her? his friend inquired.

I don't think I have, or I'd remember.

The friend went on to tell Adam all he knew about G, and where she could be seen, and when. Adam filed away the information. He was boyish, with wire-rimmed glasses and a full pink mouth which contradicted the serious frown marking his brow. He was, in style, a youthful version of G's father. The difference was etched in his mouth only, its sensuous weakness.

I'm going to marry that girl, he told his friend. Wait and see. I certainly will, was the bemused reply.

Adam snatched at his chance on a windy afternoon in Boston.
She was passing over the Mass. Ave. Bridge with her skirt flying all around while she modestly poked it down.

If middle class life is so grotesque, said Adam in her hair,
why do you want the poor to aspire to it?
Why? Who are you? she wondered.

Someone who has been listening to you and disagrees.
So leave me alone.

But I'm interested in what else you have to say about this.
Too bad. You'll never hear it.

You're not very polite.

They were stopped by a red light, side by side, backs to the
river. She glanced through her blowing hair at him.

Everyone should have the right to a decent life, she said.
That's all I'm interested in.

That sounds realistic, he stated. Why don't you let me buy
you a drink and you can explain it more?
I don't want to. That's why not.

I'm harmless.

Though bored by his seeming equanimity, by his smile as smug to her as a stuffed animal, she found something attractive in him too. It drove her at him. She felt she could say anything to him, and dodged cars to cross the street, eager to escape such liberties. He followed, talking softly and persuasively over her shoulder, and when they reached the other side of the street, she looked into his face and recognized the cold charm of his personal history. It resembled her own. For a long time she had been without the ability to love a stranger, and since you are barely alive without such an ability, she was enfeebled emotionally, all mouth and vocabulary. She strained towards the invitation he was making, and said Okay, I'll have a drink. Later.

Now, he said, and his lips beamed insistently; taking a step closer and her arm, he added, I hear you're a genius. And I know you're planning to graduate Summa a year ahead.

That's why I'm so tired, she sighed and let him steer her.

You don't look it. You look as fresh as the proverbial rose.

I'd rather be as fresh as the rose itself. Not the proverbial one.

The slope of her soft cheek and transparent green of her eye, and a smatter of freckles was all he could see through the net of her hair. She looked as if she were pushing through cobwebs in a dim room and needed guidance. He eyed her thin body with its unexpectedly high round bottom and said, I think you're the most beautiful girl I ever saw in my life. I love you.

She laughed.

Do that again.

Ha—

Can you also cry at will?

I used to, when I did skits, she said.

Do you love me?

I hate your type.

That's good. We've got something strong going already. I love you and you hate me. Great.

Forget the drink, she told him and took off down another street.

He didn't follow her, and she began to keep an eye out for him after that. Working mornings in a bookstore, then going to classes and studying until deep into the night, she still kept a half-hearted watch for him, being generally uninterested in the love of boys and men. She was, at the time, obsessed with a desire to leave Boston, and her rush through college was only a way to get out fast.

My travel plans are limited to floors.

When you love, run for your life, or suffer.

A witness in an elevator blanks out, the doors take too long to open. When a truck is on fire, the people jump over a bridge to put out the flames.

A fifteen-year warranty is too long for a weapon. Likewise seed coats, wild grain, and automobile throttles are short term.

Each subject yearns for the safety of artifice.

Humans aspire to be robots.

All music circles a secret center; its red sunset's in my hand.

When I am near one particular man, a third party made only of heat energy is created between us.

Put us twenty feet apart and that is the exact size of this third party. I can't explain the feeling, because it might be hate, though it feels like sex. No, I don't want to admit it, but I wouldn't want to live if I didn't hate.

Dear T—

Freedom is all I want. I know that now. Not to be tied down by love, family or school. To be alone and away and moving. I'll visit you en route, I promise.

Love ,

G

And this was how Adam persuaded her, finally, to get close to him. I'm driving around the country in September, he lied. You can get a free lift with me.

Adam had come up from behind, where she was complaining to a girlfriend about her lack of travel money. They were outside the bookstore as she was leaving work for the day. She whipped her head around; her hair trailed over his lips, he was so close. The sensuous mouth opened and smiled, but the gray eyes behind the glasses were still and fixed on hers. He lifted his hand into her hair, pushing it back.

See you, said the girlfriend and left.

I can promise you a free ride, he repeated. But you'll obviously have to give up the hate you feel for me. You'll have to turn it around. Are you a virgin?

Both, she replied.

Come on, I'll buy you lunch.

His hand stayed weighed in her hair. She let it lie there, as heavy as a collar. Even as they walked to the sandwich shop, she in black and he in pink, she felt a yearning for him and it was tied, frantically, with her feeling that she could verbally abuse him and get away with it. He was familiar in his clean and pressed clothes and boyish manner; he was strikingly like the father whose heat was as soft as the heat of a rose.

A relationship is fixed and frozen from almost the first moment of inception.
Breeze and sun will melt the diamond chunks of ice, but nothing can dissolve the fit of two characters.

Oars creak under ice. It's been fifty days below zero. Clandestine attentions are paid to the homeless and crazy, as to the ring of water on a barroom table.
An emptying carafe, a laugh across the room, talking about spice, hobbies, anguish over money, while others suffer and starve.
Hospital beds measure exactly the speed of my anxiety.

By the time they were married and had necked, frenziedly, their way to bed, she found she could not be satisfied. There was no resolution to her anger at him or her desire for him. Each was projected into infinity and after a while, all she wanted was his approval, but it was not forthcoming, could not be. He could not forgive her for the error which neither of them could identify. They quipped and snapped with their tongues, and craved with their bodies.

They never did leave Boston to go west, because of his work on his doctorate. Her parents rarely came to see them. They disapproved of Adam whom they called The Semitic Phase, but not to G's face. Nonetheless, she, noting their emotion, felt herself orphaned into a sore form of the freedom she had sought. The spaces between all people expanded. Finally, Adam left her for a woman he could understand, and they parted with miserable, wondering expressions.

When G got on the train that time, her appearance was ravaged, fortyish, and she had lost the connection between labor and returns, necessity and words. Some leftover energy kept her going forward, as if for a day when she would arrive at the start again, and be restored to youth. Every day felt like the last day of her life—the one day in which all the others reach fulfillment. Simple pleasure (sex or alcohol) was an important thing to remember then.

I'm not sure I'm saying the right thing.
The steel table glows in the dark. I am never able to afford the object of my desire, since the price is all my living energy, my vital parts, my attention and soul.

Once I had universal appeal. All people would confide in me. Love was no stranger. Now if I had the comic sense, I would return this heart for that earlier one.

Do you know how it feels to be a cartoon character? I don't think so.

A man who looked like Abe Lincoln often wore a tall silk hat around the house. When he got drunk, he said, Me free them? Never!

That's what it feels like.

One summer, A took the children to Verona, and Darlene too. It was the tail end of summer, and a rushed spontaneous trip. A had to get the house fixed up for some new tenants who would be renting it for months to come, and the enterprise gave her a sense of purpose which she often lacked.

She hated aging, the cruelty of the body's fattening conclusion. Her waistline thickened, even if she fasted; and menopause and dying represented her whole predictable future. Her green eyes, once illuminated by all that passed before them, now looked inwards, as if a shade were half-drawn on a sunny room.

Want to come swimming? Go for a walk with me? Get some *gelato*? Need some help with those beans? G asked Darlene again and again, because her mother seemed to want only solitude in which she could brood, like one moving into the shade on a hot day. No one could get her out to do anything. Not even T could seduce her away from the cool house and its trivial problems, which she tended to, half-heartedly, but with a pretense at their importance. She sent Darlene away with G every day, and for several hours they would roam the roads and beaches, hand in hand, mouths agape.

One day A saw the garbage man, a golden god-like Northern Italian. She watched him steadily through the curtains as he hurled trash from the end of the path into his truck, his long muscular torso bare and burning. In the midday sun, his spine was a damp shadow running between golden beams.

The next time he came back, she was out there waiting in short shorts and a little white cotton blouse tied under her fulsome breasts. She got his attention by holding up a bag of fish and laughing and saying Can you get rid of this? It stinks. In Italian.

Now A returned from a prolonged exchange with the garbage man, and her face was fiery and she had the familiar moisture in her green eyes. She said, He's very funny, and intelligent. Imagine!

What did he say that was so impressive? asked T.

Nothing, really. It was just the way he said it.

I'm sure he has a wife and six children.

Oh probably. So what?

You were flirting with him.

For God's sake Tonio. He's practically your age.

Not quite.

Why don't you go find yourself a girlfriend, instead of spying on me? I'm old and I'm married, she added.

Oh yes, I forgot, said T, coldly.

Well, you're not. Why don't you enjoy your freedom? Go and pick up some girl.

And then what? he asked and folded shut the book he was reading.

I won't say in front of Gemma. But you know perfectly well.

How do you know I haven't already?

She laughed, walking away. You sound like the person who said he didn't need to read a book, because he had already read one.

T, watching from a chair on the lawn, let out a great sigh of disgust, and G, scared, chewed her nails. She hated being caught between her mother and brother who were like emotions put into physical bodies, bodies without control, and emotions as wild as any mistral. They hissed, sighed, groaned and mused around her, always loud, always in a state of excitement, whether it was gloomy or delighted. They were drawn to each other like kitten and dog. With her father, or Darlene, G could be and see clear. But how confusing it was to be stuck between her mother and brother! She bit her nails and was always sure she must be making a mistake of some kind, when she noted falsehoods behind their deeds.

T watched her go, his eyes narrowed, and his lips. G spat her
bitten nails into the grass and tried to think up a wisecrack or a
soft word to settle the situation. But he was up and gone,
down the path to the beach, before she had fixed on the state-
ment: I hate grown-ups, except for Darlene.

A few days later T was taken away by some friends, to visit
Florence and Rome, and immediately A was taken away, too,
by the garbage man. At night. On the back of his Lambretta,
she sped away, saying to G, Don't mention this to your father
or Tonio, okay? They might misunderstand.

The word *misunderstand* then came to G as the essence of all
that was fearful in the world. She wanted to misunderstand
her own thoughts about her mother, as much as her mother
wanted to be misunderstood; yet both of them, at the same
time, wanted to be loved. If you could only love what was pre-
sented as superficially true, then you were always attached to
a set of lies, and the realities played amoral games in a chasm.
This image of the human person was also the image of the
universe.

One night G decided, bravely, to challenge that image, and she lay awake to see her mother returning with the garbage man. If they kissed, it would mean that what looked to be true was, in fact, true. She left her window open beside the bed, and the cicadas shook the air with their singing; a scent of lemon and flowers floated in. And when the lights of the scooter crossed the ceiling, she sat up and peeked out. Her throat was tight as the light went out and she saw and heard nothing but shapes in shadow. She knew if she stayed seated she would burn through the dark in her eyes and see what she felt she ought to see. But if she saw them kissing and couldn't tell anyone, what good would it do?

Her indecision for that time made her hate herself as much as she had ever hated grown-ups. Who could she hate more, the one or the other? The sound of her mother's voice settled that, and she fell back hard onto her bed, scared to trembling, because, in the end, she didn't dare know what was really so, and forgot instead.

In the morning she saw that her mother wore a puffy, satisfied look and she sensed what it meant. They were leaving in a few days for home. Will you be glad to leave, G asked her mother. Of course, was the response. The mother then eyed her daughter over the rim of her sea-blue cup and said, Paolo, the garbage man, was just a friend, as you know. Can you believe it? He's a communist!

So? wondered G because her mother usually saved her confidences for her son.

It's so interesting. Everyone, Dear, in this country seems to be either socialist or communist. I can't wait to tell Tonio. He'll be very interested. You couldn't possibly understand yet, but it's about time the working classes took some power away from the rich.

Her eyes glittered with the excitement of the newly informed and her long manicured fingers were lifted for morning inspection. They gave her permission, it would seem, to withdraw into her own private thoughts.

Wasn't Uncle Joe rich? asked G.

I guess so, said the mother without attention; then asked, What?

Nothing, never mind.

G lay her head down on her folded arms, on the table, and squinted until the shapes around the window vanished. Like a miniature screen, the window shimmered images: figures, faces, places. They were scattered and broken, though, by a hand on her neck. A soft warm squeeze and she leaned into Darlene's palm and rested there. They both looked at the mother as if she was an image cast by electricity, paint, or light on a wall beside them.

Then A became dimensional, shot forward, a sharp look at Darlene, and a sigh preceeded her words, don't mention any of this please, Darlene.

Any of what?

This question forced A back into her usual posture. She couldn't stand to be known by anyone.

My private life. Here, she said, is none of your, or anyone else's business.

Darlene gave a short laugh and moved away and G felt the currents change.

Her mother was watching Darlene with the eyes of a hater.

I can't find a courageous person outside the military or these private walls. Like a mushroom-shaped terrarium with a cloudy surface and slimy with algae, confined environments produce creatures who live a confused life.

After they returned from Italy, Darlene and Ron took G to his mother's place. It was a cold fall day and they drove over the river and out through the brick and gray of the Fenway and its nettled attempt at being pastoral. G chattered away in the back seat, excited by what seemed to her to be an enormous event; for years she had wanted to see where Ron and Darlene really lived.

When they left the trees and river, they entered into the city and passed under the el. Shadows criss-crossed the cold cement and a wintery wind blew up papers. G had the sense of familiarity which belongs more to dreams than to waking time. A psychic dread of large shapes enveloped her head and throat like a little hood worn by falcons. Ron's dark brown hand was dropped over the back of the seat and she reached out to hold onto his long fingers. He gave her hand a squeeze and she leaned forward on the seat to be closer to their voices, which were subdued precisely so she wouldn't hear them.

The woman hates me, whispered Darlene. Ever since that
sex scene in Italy.
Don't worry about it.
I have to. But he's okay, you know.
Uh uh. What passes in him for charm and goodness are some-
thing else.
Like what?
Confidence, indifference.
There's not a mean bone in his body.
Maybe not an active mean bone. But he'd let you sink before
he'd reach out to stop you from drowning. Wouldn't want to
get his hand wet. I tell you. In the white man's world, it goes:
"If you're sleeping, you're dead."
Come on. He's not so bad. He's not prejudiced.
Ha. He's the type who believes that only white men are al-
lowed to be integrationist. Watch and see. He'd never express
it, of course. Too polite. But I know. None of those liberals
are what they seem to be. They have no non-white friends,
not a one of them. They seem to think it's in such poor taste to
notice a person's race that you're better off not noticing him at
all. It's like that. I tell you.
Who are you talking about, asked G, as if she didn't know.

His mother lived in a little blue house pressed between some red brick projects and apartments. It looked across an avenue onto Franklin Park, which held the city zoo. The house, like many in New England, was very old with low ceilings and windows with small panes. The day being Sunday, the mother had prepared a large dinner for them. Several bowls of food—rice, yams, greens, ham, beef, muffins, butter—were set on a round table in the small diningroom adjoining the kitchen. Ron's four brothers and sisters and various small children lounged around the house, eating, talking, playing cards, listening to the radio, while their mother, a slow-moving woman with quick examining eyes, served the food. No one paid special attention to G, but she heard herself referred to as the little white girl more than once, and she knew that they knew she was there, seated on the edge of a red leather chair.

The children went off to play, and G stayed, listening to a discussion rising between Ron, Darlene and the older members of the family. It was all about politics and religion, about race and money. The feeling was tense in the air—that Ron was in danger and making a mistake. The mother and a sister were on the side of Jesus, and things taking time. Two of Ron's brothers were on the side of the Army and getting an education. Another sister, Darlene and Ron were on the dangerous side together, a place where their family didn't want them to be. Ron did most of the talking, trying to convince his mother, in particular, that segregation was unnatural, that "the problem in this country is economic, and if you can eliminate class, you can eliminate racism." His mother disagreed, vehemently, and spoke of the need for complete spiritual renewal. The sister who was on the same side as Ron—a tall slim woman with a serious face—tried to persuade her mother, in soft tones, that the spirit would just have to wait till the body was fed. And the two other brothers (one was in uniform) spoke of getting a foothold "in the ranks" and of hanging on hard to the system until you can claim it and call it your own.

Young as she was G sensed that she was at the heart of the world outside. The words flying around her came from a center of experience unlike any she had encountered before. The city outside was their target, but was also their arsenal. All that brick and steel, stone and speed became an image in G's mind, an image of actual emotion, the result of conflict and desire. A wall was not just a wall; it stood for a feeling. In the room she occupied for those hours was an expression of emotion intimately tied to the physical products around the people. G felt herself turn into one of those products. It had no-value, as far as she could judge, or feel.

The discussion grew hot, then soft. No one wanted to injure the mother, and Ron, constantly insisting on the last word, was finally told to shut up and sit down. He did, pulling the Sunday paper with him. Passing a section across G, to his sister, he sighed deeply. G crawled out of the chair, to sit beside him. A slight shift in his position acknowledged her presence. This undramatic move was enough to reassure her that she did after all have some value, if only the value of being alive.

Mapping and blocking my plans:
Today is Thursday, the President's birthday. My room contains exciting projects in the way of explosives.
Wood fires are like parents, the fractions combine to make one burn. I've already had a father, and while one is alive, you can't have two.
In my part of town the stores are closed due to an overturned oil truck.

Divinity, engulf my tremors.
If you want to be great, you must serve the guilty and the lost without judgment.

On another Sunday Ron and Darlene had driven G back home after lunch and were unusually silent on the way. This signified to G their reluctance at leaving the family scene behind and each other. She wanted to make the inevitable easier for them, but could only produce a couple of false smiles, at best, from Darlene.

Who could have given the information, Ron wondered aloud, and why? I don't have any enemies I know of.

G's continuing love for Ron, a big man who smiled rarely, made her particularly sensitive to his moods. She could interpret his breath and speech patterns and his gestures without difficulty. He and Darlene separated awkwardly at the back door, and only after murmured reassurance of their next meeting. And G looked away, into the snow-blue trees, and the stars, waiting for him to kiss her goodnight, which he always, and now, did.

The mother was waiting in the kitchen. The father was out at some meeting. And as she had been at home all day, A wore a flushed expression, her hair uncurling in places. Tension hid her lips. How was it, she asked, but didn't wait for an answer. Go upstairs, she told G who passed, obediently, through the swinging door but there paused to listen.

You've got to leave tomorrow, Darlene, said the mother.
What? Why?
Because of Ron.
But why?
You know why.
I don't.
You do. And just take my word for it. You have to go.

Branches creaked beside the pantry window, and old leaves, stuck around from the fall, crackled in the window frame. G stood still among the shelves and dishes.

The FBI spoke with my husband last night.

Oh, it's because— ! cried Darlene.

Yes.

And he told them his name, his address?

They know everything. He had to tell them. It's the law. . . . Darlene, you can't take risks like this. You're a Negro, and as if that's not bad enough, Ron is a party member. You're associating with a Communist.

Associating, Darlene responded: Associating!

At least you can't while you work for me.

Well, I don't anymore. That's for sure.

Don't speak to me like that. Remember your place, said the mother, and as her clipping heels approached the door, G fled.

She ran up to her room and her bed, and hid there alone. Though she tried, she couldn't make sense of that scene, but she knew there was no one around to comfort anyone in it. No one inside the house, or outside the house. No one in the world. The cold finality of the operation gave her her first contact with separation. Enforced. In one hour her idle and contented gaze turned into a look of scrutiny, sometimes suspicion, and even though she forgot that experience, in its specifics, she watched her parents differently afterwards—with the eyes of a guard one day, the eyes of a prisoner the next. Darlene was gone before the sun was up, and G would never locate her or Ron again, though looking often in passing faces for theirs. This search, even as it became unconscious over the years, let her see beyond the attributes of race into the particularities of a face. The search in this way was subversive.

There are animated bodies other than my own, but I can't really know them without love.

This is the horror. All I guess is, by the time I've touched someone, we've both moved on, and loneliness puts us each into perpetual motion.

The city is all one color because snow is on the way.

It has an appearance of absolute stone. Houses look rejecting, clubby, with their windows and their smoke.

Being rejected is actually freeing. You can love in peace.

In 1962 G drove to the Committee on Racial Equality in Roxbury where she was working voluntarily, interviewing, chasing down slumlords. The sun was blazing through the windows of the car. As she passed up Columbus Avenue under the el on Washington Street, her eyes took in the sights: trembling heat waves emerging from concrete and steel; shadows bearing down like enormous claws from above; children playing with rocks, bottles on the sidewalk, their clothes shabby both from oversoiling and overwashing.

At a set of lights, she lurched into gear, feeling her own solitude unfold like the opening leaves in a camera lens, one after the other, leading nowhere. Shit, she whispered, sensing the imminence of an anxiety attack. She kept driving, hunched over, with the awareness of annihilation coming closer, a literal natural force, rolling down those ruined streets.

The judgment of God, like a lion's paw, seems to get its weight from its other parts resting firmly on the ground, elsewhere. She stopped the car in the sharp shadows under the el, a train broke through the silence overhead. *Divorce, divorce,* was the word in her head. Divorce, and *worse, mortal, torn, divide, unborn.* . . . And she leaned down her head, the engine rumbling against her feet, and her mind was led by words, one after another, away from the safety of its own control, but spilling forth, as if pressed upon to bursting. Little flashes of resistance, which she held up like shields before them, were flattened at once. The words became nasty, and cruel *(schizoid, paranoid, autistic, catatonic, psychotic)*, the opposite of Hope Chest, the dowry of her divorce.

She turned off the engine. She was now on Blue Hill Avenue, a ravaged strip of commerce running straight from downtown Boston toward the suburban hills. Dark faces glittered from the heat moisture. She stared at them all, deep breathing, and tossing back those words with an attempt at wit, at nonchalance. *Psychosis, depression:* enervating terms with which humanity described itself. And she couldn't laugh.

The white sky blanketed the curvature of earth, and the jutting hardline buildings. The solid people all seemed to have been shaken down out of that blanket, cast down from its soft center. The images in her eyes, these, came from miles away. What does it mean? Why have we all been spilled down on the ground, for this?

Ruined buildings, fallen flesh and the litter of a civilization strewn out in long term decay: nothing good flickered on the screen in her vision, but behind them was an emanation, a memory of emotion, of a time when the word and the thing were one and the same. To be saved by a word! To be healed by a word: would be to be uplifted, from under that weighted paw. Fear was her disease, expecting a word like love or charity to cure her.

But the first word was despair and it sailed into her vocabulary, like a tall ship from some haunted other time, tilting over a cold ocean. Despair, she realized, is what I'm feeling. It's an ancient feeling, and is born in each person. Despair, the word, came like a sweet-dropping medicine, a coat of taste for her fear. Never had a word had such reverberating power for her. Never had one word been so strong it could humiliate all the little psychological bits and pieces, those labels that peeled off like slogans in a long rain.

She huddled on the sticky plastic seat of her father's old Ford, her hands squeezing the steering wheel, her whole mind and mouth centered on the word that made rebellion as inevitable as the hell it hated.

Everyone only wants to get home to bed, where things begin and end. If you shut your eyes and stretch out your arms, even then you can't get rid of your body. The affiliation is morally binding. The body has more sides than the moon. Is it really my own?

Bubbling springs force water onto a dry and distant tongue. So do feathery cream cakes and sweet black nibs of chocolate. But whoa. Hold the pleasure. I forgot the world had seductive offerings to make. I forgot that love was pleasure.

In the inconclusive book that P was planning to write, there was nothing ahead for Western civilization but plague and trouble. When he first imagined the book he set out to prove that self-interest, the perverse child of Emerson's self-reliance, was responsible for social problems. But as his eyes widened on the issues of poverty and decay, and his conservatism increased, and his need to keep his liberal associations remained stable, he grew confused, and lost sight of an argument. Absolute pragmatism is our only hope, he would state one day; the next he would say, Absolute pessimism is the only perspective on civilization's ills.

Come on, his wife would groan. Don't be such a poop. The world isn't going to end. Not while we're around anyway.

Maybe not, but soon after, he said glumly.

Then what will we care? she asked.

All this work? For nothing?

What work?

Michelangelo, Shakespeare, Einstein . . . That work.

That work! she screamed from her place in her nightgown. Why always the famous people? Why always the big guns? Why always the people who have it all? Why always the men? That work! Einstein? What about a garbage man's work, what about a ditch digger's work, what about the work of the people who built the Globe theater, what about the women who gave birth to them? You ass! I hate you! Michelangelo, Einstein, Shakespeare! What about their wives and their children? What about the people who nobody ever notices! I'm so sick of it, so sick of all of you, pompous sons of bitches, I want out, I want to get out, I've got to get out, let me OUT!

The father sat on the edge of the bed, in striped pajamas, speechless. She had never had an outburst before, so he sensed it was somehow critical, and he should be afraid. And indeed, within days, she was gone—to Italy, to her new home.

There is no longer any class outside the class of character, and no history to put your faith in.

You can actually live as if you have no culture, no perspective particular to a date in time.

You are an individual whose prime and solitary property is your own body.

Dying becomes a hell beyond all reason or justice in this ahistorical context.

I don't know where I came from. Did that old body belong to me? Am I the same one—frail, unsheltered? This, an offering to the world?

Two feet a day.

Like fragile cologne, a spill can spark violence, a fast-moving storm, a spiderweb from a tickled belly—thin but strong.

If the going is easy, you're not traveling.

Substitute energy for irony, be kind to your head and submerge it.

When A left him, the father's somber face was justified. He lost his appetite, he cried, alone, at night. His ability to perform helped him to continue, superficially the same, through the days, playing tennis, talking about budgets, searching for new funds, rattling off pleasantries and platitudes that amused the secretaries who loved him. He assured everyone it was not a divorce, or even a separation, but a long-needed change for his wife. They both loved Italy, and he would join her there in the summer. And these statements were true enough so that even he could learn to live with them, and with her gone, after his suffering was exhausted. But one form of hope had left him permanently with her departure. It was the hope that he would, one day, understand human nature.

In the collapsible house of origins, water leaks through snapped plaster. Lathing shows lines that are really black air. The tiles are dust around the fireplace. The outside walls, wooden, brown, have settled at the edges of the ground and curl up from it.

Nature demands expression from us, strangely, yet my will is a machine. Separating adjacent facts turns meaning into accident, so there seems to be only a comic law left, emanating from each act and fact.

My body is sunk in sensation when in bed, and the geometry of its hope is found in opposites.
I want each part of my body to be united with another, unlike it, and to find rest like this.

G's virginity had gone to Adam, and after she left him a couple of times she tried to see if sexuality's proximity to love might cure her terrible sieges of depression. But they didn't heal her at all. Once, after sleeping with someone, she asked herself, How can I be happy if there is no divine scheme? And she sighed shadows. Inside the child she was stirred restlessly, as if in a bundle of swaddling clothes, but she only covered it further.

In a while she became very close to someone at the newspaper where she worked on copy. He was a father of three and already the proposed husband-to-be of another woman, since his recent divorce. G didn't know about the other woman and he certainly didn't tell her. He was a person who lived in the future, fussing and making plans, in order to allay a fundamental anxiety about the uncertain nature of his own character moving through the world. Since he couldn't predict himself, he would predict the world. He was robust, heavy-drinking, a poet and journalist who called himself a Marxist, too, and who wrote a column in that weekly paper. His friends were like hers: vehement rebels, some with red bandanas and Van Gogh beards who seemed unable to remember or experience pleasure. Unlike G and her man.

The first time he sat beside her, in a parked car, she was aware of a supernatural heat arising around them and merging somewhere between. Cliches like "I'm on fire," or "It's bigger than both of us," captioned her responses. When his sleeve brushed her hand, she "melted." It was like coming upon great art after browsing in mediocre galleries; the recognition of what was extreme annihilated all in-betweens. She looked at him as if he were personal destiny embodied in the flesh, and as if she must say, "I give up."

In actual expression it took the form of sex. They spent two-thirds of their time engrossed in each other's bodies in bed, and the other third of the time figuring out how to get there. She was horrified by the wideness of his sex appeal, but he swore to her that she, of them all, was the best, the special. Reassuring her did not require much work on his part, the inevitability of their physical attachment was so undeniable. She was happy almost all the time, and felt her self was true at last, not an invention.

His friends discussed anarchy, socialism, violence and smoked grass, which made them passive. Some took LSD and ended up in mental hospitals. They were all penniless and enraged by the forces of law and order which surrounded them. Jazz and poetry were their cultural passions. The women were quiet and cat-like, moving around edges in tatters and sandals. The centerpieces on many tables were fat heaps of candlewax.

G's man was naturally happy and he exuded a paternal warmth which she sank into. She was attracted to his size, smell, humor and weakness for alcohol. They drank together, had sneaky sex in his foul apartment, talked politics and poetry until he had to make a choice and chose the other woman. Lying to G, he said he was returning to his wife because of the children.

She didn't fight to keep him but cried a great deal. He said he wished she'd get mad instead of just sad like that, and he accused her of acting like a victim instead of a consenting adult. She threw a dish that held a burning candle and old wax—red, yellow and thick—at his face; it missed and he left, shaking his head at her violence. Later she had terrible cramps and something resembling a miscarriage, or maybe it was one. She would never know.

How did this happen? It sickens and terrifies me not to know.
If you haven't understood something by the time it's over, you
probably won't. Why didn't I notice I was doing something
wrong?
I did, but instantly swallowed each insight with further
misunderstanding.

How long can I stay here, where I don't dare be happy?
When will my number be up and will I see it flash in the trees
ahead of me?
Success is an attribute belonging to someone else, not to me.
Often when I say something intelligent, a man will say *No*, and
then restate what I just said, in his own words.

Boston is a red brick fortress where the smell of the sea gives a tantalizing but false impression of a city at liberty. Between leopardskin whores and tea at the Ritz the light is as irregular as that from a furnace-burner. Among dripping spigots and gargoyles several stories high over the Common, people are judged according to class, race and beauty. There are many cliques, and few spill into the next at the edges. Success is both despised and revered in this city. You have a better chance of surviving it if you get it elsewhere and arrive in Boston already launched as a winner. If you get it here, the enemy factor can be overwhelming. Hate is right near the surface and the old institutions are immovable. Failure is the best show in town and pleasure comes only when you can hide with it. Boston rejects its own offspring, vomits each child out onto the pavement and watches him or her crawl through the shadows toward some poor sort of survival. No helping hands are offered. The most prejudiced body of people are the most powerful, though that body switches nationality once every couple of generations. The city is a hell for the weak, or the wild.

Because she was poor at making a living and pitied her father too, G lived in his house. Every day going to work from there, she crossed boundaries that were switched by vehicles of construction and deconstruction, none of which concealed the divisions being erected. Streets were torn up and buildings were torn down. One day a store was there, the next week it was gone. Whole areas of business were obliterated, leaving a racetrack for cars to speed and smash up along, coming in and out of downtown Boston. In the winter these areas filled up with heaps of white and gray snow; in summer they trembled with trash.

At home G pretended to be necessary to her father who hardly noticed her at all. They only spoke to argue about politics. No, he replied to every suggestion of an idea coming from her.

   No, he said. Not so. The failure of Russia to live up to the revolution is the biggest failure of this century. Not capitalism. No. Russia has single-handedly poisoned every possibility of international understanding.

But you can't deny that capitalism is inefficient at the very least.

   No. Capitalism doesn't work, no, but it's not because it's inefficient.

Why then?

   Because certain valuable parts of society are not being used.

She stared at him, then, with her eyes darkened by a frown of confusion.

Once a smooth and charming talker, P now rambled on and on. G noted, in him, a rising to the surface of the submerged patrician and it made her uneasy as if she, too, might have such a person hidden inside. He was asked out to dinner endlessly, now that he served the function of being an extra man; but his pre-sleep actions and sighs gave his loneliness away. While G and he slipped past each other, night and day, four former African colonies became free nations, voter registration among blacks in the South increased by the thousands, and schools were integrated.

The powerful only talk to the powerful, Ron had said more than once. So we must only talk to the powerless.

At an early age and rapt in my own thoughts, I quaffed cheap wine and hired myself to a circus of sorts. A padded house of illusions. Like a provincial violin playing in a noisy gallery, my thoughts were cheap and feverish.

Ghosting these shores my ancestors left behind their desperation and little else. It was this I inherited. Desperate desires— for recognition, for a home.

They left however no net with which to catch a person falling away from the will to power. And without it, all that's left is the hard wooden world of the poor.

One day P woke up and P was for Poet. He said he knew it all along. It was just a matter of time. P wrote poetry suddenly; seated at his desk visions of candelabra and cards and stars all came together in a stream of logic belonging only to him. He called it Verse. It was very formal metrically. Puzzling; but suggested an intelligence caught in a garden net; a bit of a struggle, the mind thrashing among raspberries and lettuces, but made cozy by context. He had never been so happy nor felt so justified. His verse was published, too, by people who owed him favors and who genuinely enjoyed his harmless words. The lateness of his muse's arrival made him an original. He was, indeed, like one in love—humming, whistling, walking quickly. And he swore his previous life had been a preparation for these days. He saw one personal pattern where before he saw a mess. He told G, All the events which seemed beyond my control were acts of Destiny leading me, blindfolded, to my muse's door. It's extraordinary! There is an order, after all! I don't know what to name it, or where it comes from, but isn't it wonderful?

Soon after losing the bearded Marxist, G entered the subway station which blasted up heat, as from the mouth of a dog. It was late July and early evening, and a Sunday. G's face wore the preoccupied and lively look it got when she was thinking about two things at once and in opposition. One was funny, the other was a nightmare. Most of her spoken jokes were self-deprecating and could easily lead into the closet of comedy where skeletons are strung up like a row of suits.

The platform was empty but for her and four young white men, circling around a youngish black man. It looked like a game, because the white ones were laughing and jumping around like kids, but there was no mistaking the serious fear on the black man's face. He was not dressed shabbily, but in a gray business suit; he had no defense. Two of the whites held up half-empty bottles of beer. She could hear in the distant tunnel the sound of the train, and with a feverish sensation covering her skin, she shouted out, Leave him alone!

She might as well have been a ghost or a gust of wind, because they went on shouting epithets at the man, and trying to grab a hold on his shoulders. He was quick. His fear made him fast, and vicious, and he struck out successfully three times, but then he lost all vitality as they went in on him as a pack.

G seemed to leap through light years, to melt into a hard thing, propelled without thought, forward. She was enraged, and fear-less for those few seconds, throwing herself into the group of men, who were distracted by her clumsy force. They were trying to pick up the man as a group and to heave him, with shouts of one, two, three, onto the tracks beside the platform. Each could hear the train in the tunnel and the sound of its roar was all-engulfing within those stony walls.

G's anger took her over, and she kicked and used her fists on the bare flesh, their arms lifted, their faces, laughing, until it was too late for them to do as they wanted, and they threw the man in the grey suit on the ground, kicked him, and ran back out of the station . . . just as the train pulled in.

G was shaking from her knees to the top of her head. She watched a handful of people pass, pausing to look at the man getting to his feet, to brush himself off, and straighten his tie. Someone asked her if she was all right. She nodded, and as those others retreated, and the train pulled out, she became terrified, all the anger departed, and she started after the small group of commuters quickly, only wanting human company, in case those four should return. Her breathing was not automatic, too high in her chest.

At the top of the stairs the night air was mild, and black trees blew silhouettes against a yellow-grey city skyline. The Boston Common was there, few people around, and few stores lighted. Still frightened, she headed for a row of taxis when a hand on her shoulder made her lurch forward and start to run.

He said *Wait* with an accent, and she turned to see the small-ish man in the grey suit, his lips cut, his cheek scraped, and one eye puffy, trying to smile. Thank you, he said several times, and asked to know what he could do to repay her.

Nothing, nothing, it's okay.

But you're shaking.

So are you.

Not like you. Your knees!

Forget it.

I can't.

I just want to go home. Really.

Let me take you. In a cab. Please.

Around them headlights beamed and passed, and they kept a distance of several feet between them. She could tell he was African, but that was all.

All right, she relented, walking forward with him after.

My name's Augustine, he said. I was just on my way to Harvard Square, you know? Then these men came out of nowhere and jumped me. I never had an experience like that, not even at home. And I owe my life to you.

Together they climbed into the back seat of a yellow cab, and she told the driver to take them to Harvard Square. She didn't want to talk. And not, even, to listen, she was still so shaken by what had happened. All along the streets she scanned the faces for the four white men, and even into the passing cars, afraid they might find her, and enact some vengeance.

The man was quiet now, himself, and dabbing at his wounds with a handkerchief. He, too, stared out the car windows as they glided around the corners of the Common toward Beacon Street and Storrow Drive, along the river. Both their faces shone in the sweat of the night, and hers was dark with a summer tan. She unrolled the window and her black curls blew up and away from her neck.

He suddenly gasped, laughed and said loudly, I'm alive!
      Yes, you are, she agreed.
What is your name? I owe my life to you, I do.
      You already said that, but you don't, said G.
Then what do I owe it to?
      Luck, the subway coming at the right moment, I don't know.

She didn't look in his direction the better to analyze the mystery of the event, and its loneliness. What stunned her was the sensation of having been there at all, of having nothing to do with it, of blacking out, in a sense, for those seconds of violence rebounding from her. The intelligent and restrained self, her self, with whom she identified night and day, was simply not present during that time. To be praised, then, for taking action made no sense at all. No rational decision had been made; she had physically reacted in a way she was utterly unprepared for.

> If I had been in one of my nervous moods, she told him, I would have run the other way. Luckily, for you, I was feeling good.

Yes, indeed.

> What happened anyway?

Don't ask me. I don't know, you know? As I say, I was just waiting for the train, when they came up behind me. That's all.

She noted he was smiling, now, with his voice as well as his face, and she smiled back. He tipped back his head and laughed, and she laughed, too, their faces to the windows and wind blowing in.

On the streets, in Harvard Square, they stood around, then headed for a brightly lighted cafeteria, where the few faces turned to watch them as they passed. Inside they got tea, slopped onto a plastic tray, and sat at the plateglass window.

I come from southern Africa, he told her, from Durban, to be exact. I don't know if you know anything about Africa.

Not much.

Well, I was schooled by Episcopalians, which is why I speak English, you know?

Yes, I wondered.

Here I'm studying international law, actually.

Really, she murmured, hanging over the heat of her cup.

Do you want to give me your name?

G went ahead and gave it to him, her whole name, finding nothing to fear in someone who came from so far away and with whom she could laugh so easily.

He, meantime, thought she was a person of color, meeting her that night with her August tan high on her arms, legs and face, and her kinky hair flying.

You must be West Indian. Or Cape Verdean maybe?
    Why do you say that?
Well, your skin tone, you know. You must be of mixed blood?

G looked down at her arm lying on the formica table top. It was coffee brown, the same to the tips of her fingers, and she wondered at this fact, saw it as a surprise, and looking up at his smile, she couldn't resist the lie: a small reward, or gift, to herself, from her future.

My mother is West Indian, she said with a big joking smile.
She lives in—um—Barbados.
And your father?
Here! I live with him.
He must be of English extraction?
That's right.
Can I walk you home, Gemma, he asked then.
No, no, it's nearby, don't bother.
Well, I'd like to see you again, to take you somewhere a bit nicer than this, you know?
Oh you don't have to do that.
No. I want to.
I don't know, she murmured vaguely and gaped at the window, trying to think up an excuse.
I'll tell you what. I'll be outside here on Saturday night, at six. If you want to join me for dinner, do. If not, I'll understand.
That's nice of you. Okay!

They beamed at each other, and she took account of his face now, and his frame: compact, with neat, rounded features, pursed lips and hands both elegant and able. She was not much smaller than he, which contributed to a sense of ease for her. They parted outside the restaurant with him tactfully refraining from asking which way she was walking, or where she lived, and she walked aimlessly by the rough bricks of Brattle Street, under heavy perfumed leaves, talking to herself and smiling.

Time is adjusting my accounts. I wish I could re-ship all the injuries I sent out and could see them travel twice as fast by return and blow up in my hands.

Relationships constantly reach crisis points, but around this place everyone has "seen it all before." Biblical parables are rarely used by revolutionaries, but personal memories serve as illustrations. I wish I could be one.

Mental torment is hidden in the underground. Let me, too, slip into the absolute night, with faith pinned bright as starlight on my heart. Faith in childhood, that is.

They went, that Saturday night, to a French restaurant on Beacon Hill. There was a small courtyard for outside eating, with white wrought-iron tables and birch trees studded with Christmas lights. For a while they talked the usual, about Cuba, Kennedy, Communism, poverty in Boston, slumlords, the Welfare system and the domino theory; and meantime G was being affected by the lie she had told him. Deception made her pity Augustine as a victim, hers, and the pity in turn made her feel more at ease with him than she did with most people. Pity made her empathize with him, wholeheartedly, while being herself—if only at surface—a person of color made her distant from but likable to herself. When the subject turned to race, she was almost ready for it.

Did your mother and father have difficulty, as a mixed couple, in this country? asked Augustine.

Uh, yes, of course! They lived a pretty isolated existence without many friends between them. His family wouldn't speak to him again after he married her. They were horrified.

His family? What about hers? asked Augustine, as if surprised that she would only register the reaction of the white family.

Oh well, I don't really know. They were off in the West Indies, what was left of them.

I see. And for you? The child, or children?

Children. My brother and I. We were proud of it, our heritage.

No one teased or was cruel to you?

Only sometimes, she said quickly and sought to change the subject. It's hard to talk about.

She looked into the Christmas bulbs with a kind of restless twist to her shoulders.

He asked if she had ever been in love.

Once, yes, she admitted and her eyes flashed at the thought of the man.

What happened?

He went back to his wife and children.

Ah. That's bad. Loving someone married, I mean. Especially if you're not married too. I always heard a married man should only have affairs with married women, and vice versa. This way each person has love to return to, when that one ends.

That's very cynical, she said.

I don't think so at all. . . . Ideally, however, one should not have any affairs, with or without a married person.

All I know is, I was happy when we were together, and I can't imagine it would ever repeat with anyone else.

Was he black or white?

She told him white and now he paid particular attention to the shape of his fork. He turned it up and around in the light, examining the notches and grooves in its flat fake silver.

You know what I think constitutes happiness, he asked; she shook her head. When you can lie down in the night, knowing you told the truth, you did your work and you're able to love. . . . And you know what I think constitutes pleasure? Again she shook her head, but this time it was a flinch. Ha! Lying; not having to work; and only riding on the tops of people, using them, you know? It's very simple. Why then do people confuse happiness with pleasure?

The circuits. Get crossed.

True, he agreed, they do.

He could become serious and distant unexpectedly. Augustine was the first man she had met who believed in God and the divinity of Jesus. She questioned him, a lot, and with hunger, about that, and this attention from her increased their bond, so that this particular evening was one she remembered in detail. She remembered the date, the hour and the weather of that night as if the facts contributed, at last, to the meaning of the occasion.

After dinner, they walked for several lonely blocks, in the warm summer air, to the combat zone where there was a nightclub called Slade's Paradise. It was a sleazy spot with a long bar down one side, and tables and a stage on the other. Primarily a black club, frequented by the occasional white sailor or student out on a lark, it was not unsafe for whites to go there, in 1962, because the division was too complete to cross with even the contact of violence.

G and Augustine danced in the style of the times, not touching, but circling close, bending at the knees and lifting up again; and then they watched a female group sing and gesticulate in gold lamé dresses, hair straightened and bobbed. The club was hot and filled with those foresexual smells of alcohol, sweat and smoke. G observed Augustine less intelligently now, and more with the desire of a twentyish woman who is ready to be filled with love and children, a little desperate at the nerve ends, but still selective, cautious. His small, tense frame in a herringbone suit and slow-moving hands made her eyes spark and moisten, like her mother's years before, so she leaned in close to this man waiting for him to touch her. He didn't. Not there, not on the streets and not even when she dropped him at his building, before driving back to hers. He just thanked her for the evening and promised to call. When she went inside, she breathed the air as if it were a liquor that could pass into her body, and give it a rush of emotion. For something, in her, was missing, only to be replaced by something lesser and lighter.

It was a few weeks before Augustine phoned G again. He had moved into Boston, and she went to see him, crossing a border between red brick townhouses and waves of newly poured tar to a strip of stores—hair stylist, coffee shop, wholesale meat, bargain outlet, Tae Kwon Do studio, flophouse and liquors—over which he lived. She would cross this border, back and forth, many times, in her visits to see him, whose apartment windows rattled from the nearby elevated trains. His white curtains, white as sails in the sun when she first saw them, soon grew grey, blowing in and out of the screenless windows.

The first time she went to his apartment it was with the flushed anticipation of physical love. Sex with him would affirm the lie that she was a person of color, and would then set her on a fresh course, a liberation she longed for. She had no doubt of his desire for her, and her internal organs felt as red and fresh as roses shaking in drops of rain and sun. Warmth traveled the stem of her spine. She breathed from her abdomen, knocking on his scraped and cracked door. When she saw him, she was both hot and shy. Immediately she sank onto his sofa, waiting for the rest to follow. He handed her a cup of tea on a saucer.

It's wonderful to see you, he told her.

You too.

She imagined herself with her soft brown skin and black curls pulled into a pony tail like someone from some old Southern novel. She smiled in a way that would be called demure, and tilted in his direction. He wore his shirt sleeves rolled above his elbows, and smoked a small cigarillo. He talked about his home and said:

I'm engaged to a woman who is now living in Geneva. We will be married as soon as I've finished school.

He leaned out and took a book off the side table. In it was pressed a photo of his fiancee, a smiling African woman, who looked, to G, like a student, too, with a sweater and blouse neatly buttoned and a bookshelf behind her. He looked at this image as if it were alive; he was smiling into it.

What's her name? Tell me about her, said G and he told her while her temples and throat throbbed less with disappointment than with embarrassment.

After this day she entered the rest of the season with his friendship central to the system of her time, her work, her new image. Her lie about her race made her see the world fresh the way you do on the first October day which is clear and blue. Each green leaf sustained the shadow of another green leaf—a black cut-out. The pavement glittered with a mica unnoticed before, and squirrels ate nuts with focused relish. Grains of sugar seemed larger than ever; cream was sweeter; and the smell of the air anywhere was human and familiar. It was like being in love with the new person that she now was.

G, liberated from the sense of being on the wrong side of history, let her freedom carry her forward into territories where she forgot herself. She cross-examined Augustine and others on African colonialism and literature, in the effects of oppression and racism on the Third World, and so on. Her ignorance accompanied her to parties with Augustine, where foreign and Afro-American students got together around midnight to eat and dance and talk. She questioned people left and right, unaware that her curiosity was making many turn away from her, wondering, suspiciously, what her background was. Into that winter she often worked with Augustine in his small but immaculate studio with the gray curtains hanging over smudged glass. He was a person fixated on one goal—to leave the United States with a degree in law, expertise he would use closer to home. He was not very interested in gossip—about G, in particular, towards whom he was instead protective.

In January she left her father's house and moved into the same building as Augustine. She took a studio apartment two floors below him and supported herself writing articles for the local papers, working on housing violations for the Congress of Racial Equality and typing for people, mostly students she met with Augustine. She was living, now, within walking distance of the hospital where T was treated for asthma; and she was also within walking distance of Ron's mother's house. She passed under the shadows of the el daily and climbed its iron stairs to go to work, and to look across the rooftops of brick flophouses toward a bunched-up downtown Boston. In the fertility of a life lost to prosperity, she was happy.

A failure of faith is at the heart of a failure of nerve.

On Primary Day I wore heavy tweeds in the still-warm weather. Political placards swung to and fro as I ran down the center of the main street, stopped traffic.

My mother wanted to give the physician information about me, and my economic situation and the sadness I felt. I told her it was unfulfilled sexual desire being transferred into grief, and this stopped her from taking that drastic and embarrassing step.

Those who have suffered severe displacement and separation really have no need for more suffering. They have, instead, a fear of all new events and only crave an end to drama and change. For this they are called lazy and irrelevant.

Many people who are professional believe that in the end you have no standard of value available to you but your own and since they have power, you must do as they say. The process is called axiology.

Mothers everywhere bite their nails, pull their hair and cry when they remember their pleasures.

G only recognized the danger she was in when her brother came to see her, unexpectedly. He laid his back against the wall and sprawled on her single bed, frowning. He patted the bed. She sat beside him and prayed that none of her friends would call on her now. If they saw T, they would know at once that she wasn't what she said she was. Even with his healthy tan, he was unmistakably the product of a privileged white family.

Mother wants you to go to Italy, he told her, and to spend some time there alone, or with her, in the house. I think it's a good idea. You can't live like this. . . . We don't live like this.

Like what? she asked, genuinely curious.

He waved toward the window, where frost was bulging inside the glass, and toward the ceiling, cratered and stained.

Come on, Gemma, you know what I mean.

No. You don't understand, she told him, how happy I am. I'm on my own, but I have lots of friends.

What friends?

Never mind, let's go out, she said, threatened by the vision of her friends entering with the lie she had given them. But he stayed solidly still.

You've always had friends. What about a man?
Not right now, no.

You should get married, settle down.
I will, but I'm still young.

Don't marry someone poor, please.
She examined his handsome face, now narrower and tighter
like his father's, but with the full lips and brown skin they
shared. He spent so much time, these days, in snow and sun,
he was very dark. To her his face was so familiar it was like
some famous impressionist print you see in every bookstore.
It was fixed in time like that, outside of possible injury.

Just because you married someone rich and glamorous, it
doesn't mean I have to, too.

I'm just telling you what Mother asked me to tell you.
As if I'd listen.

Well, I told her I'd say it. Anyway, at least come out and
have dinner with me. Come on. I'll pay for everything.

They went to an Italian restaurant in the North End. She wore a ratty fur coat, purchased in a junk shop, and galoshes with buckles. Her frizzy hair was pinned down with barettes, making her face, over its wide bones, show every shift in expression, more than she knew. She ate like a pig and guzzled wine cheerfully, while T told her about his sexual and other adventures. He worked as a ski instructor in Italy most of the time, was married to a Swiss woman, was bisexual and constantly pushing himself to extremes, physically. He didn't read much any more, but loved the opera and the ballet. His red mouth, greased against chapping, twisted often into a bemused expression, suggesting he was ready for anything. He talked about their mother, intimating that she was silly and beneath contempt.

I haven't seen her for ages, said G. I don't know what she's up to anymore, and I don't much care.
You can't be that callous. It doesn't suit you.

Well, I have nothing in common with her, or Father. I feel I was born into the wrong family, it was a terrible mistake on the part of Fate.
No. I look into your eyes and you're still my little sister. Why have you chosen such a dreary life though, why? Here you have money and this glorious Italian house at your disposal. Loosen up! Be more Mediterranean and not such a Puritan.

As she used to, G felt a slight waver of excitement in her, just at the force of his presence, and she almost confided in him, about her false identity, about her lie she was calling her life. The words hovered in front of her lips, and emanated a kind of gravity that she wanted to resist. She put food in her mouth and drank to keep herself from speaking, and as she did so, she was aware of the enormity of the lie and also of its absurdity. It even occurred to her that maybe everyone knew she was white, and that the lie was being reversed back onto her. Like looking in two mirrors—one behind, and one in front—excessive perspectives wheeled in the air around her. If she clapped shut one of the mirrors, the image would vanish, but not what it had showed. That would stay, attached to the actual physical body she occupied, the one she labeled "colored" when it should have read "white."

I see you still love your wine, said T. More? Why don't you live with me, or someone like me?

My God, said G.

Shocked? I'll let you do anything you want.

G had changed color, seeing the bearded journalist—his name was Dieter (said like "Peter")—enter the restaurant with a woman. His beard, graying, and his streaked blond hair, smoothed back from a high white forehead, made him look older than she remembered. He wore a black three-quarter-length overcoat she would know by its smell.

Who's that? asked T.

A man I hate.

Looks more like love to me.

Dieter pushed the woman aside toward the cloak room then, and came to G's side.

Where are you living now? he asked.

In Boston.

I'll find you, he said. Don't worry.

And he walked, confident and smiling, to another table.

What an awful man, T remarked. How did he know I wasn't your lover? What is he—sexy?

I guess.

You don't need that kind of man. He looks like he stepped out of a Swedish movie about the Black Plague. Come home and sleep with me instead. Wouldn't that be the fulfillment of our most secret desires?

No, it wouldn't, she told him. You really are disgusting.

Not in bed. I can show you.

He was as serious as he could ever be, and she was too. When he got her home, she ran in alone and slammed the door as if he was chasing her. Then she grabbed a bottle of cheap burgundy and listened down the hall to hear if anyone was home. Off at a distance she heard music and laughter, and she hesitated. She was in a high state of excitement. Part of it came from the fear of being discovered as a fake in the presence of her brother, and in his wake; the other part came from seeing the man she loved and hearing his promise to find her. If he did as he said, however, he might expose her lie to those friends down the hall (all under thirty and none of them rich, or white), just by being with her. She ventured into the hall and, bottle in hand, passed one open door, where there was no music but voices, past another, where there was music and no voices. She climbed the stairs to where two students shared one small apartment exactly like hers, and the door was open, and a crowd was assembled inside. Smoke veiled the door. She paused, feet away from the entrance, overcome with consciousness not of the lie, but of the truth. She had no right of access into those areas; she was not really close to anyone but Augustine; she was a reverse subversive and as homeless as she deserved to be. She returned, then, to her apartment, alone with her embarrassment.

Nature's intention sometimes seems to be the reverse of her results, that intention being that all should be forgotten, that there should be no trace of a physical event. Sometimes it seems that the pulse of all living creatures comes from a voluntary rebellion against the supreme intention, which longs for emptiness or only the rub of wind against wind. Sometimes all the varieties of wildflower, fern, pool and sea seem to spring from subversion, the genius of the spirit in disguise, as it struggles against that omnivore, nature herself. In this way the spirit becomes the enemy of the world, but fits itself to her forms, and hides there, inside her, holding her together.

The minute Dieter entered her rooms, G took him back. She fell into his arms when he held them out, overwhelmed by the kindness of a destiny that returned him to her. It was a chilly afternoon, and he told her he was free for her alone, he was free for good. In his briefcase he carried a bottle of scotch and a bar of chocolate-covered caramel she particularly liked. He was writing, on commission for a respectable publisher, a book about charity in America, he told her, as they drank their way toward her bed.

    I hate the way I feel so outside my subject, he said. As soon as you move into big-time publishing, you lose that visceral contact—the kind I can see you have—with the underdog.
Why do you want it, she inquired.

    For the book. So it will ring true.
He laid her back, then, and set to removing her clothing with the authority of one who has been there before.

In spite of G's efforts to spend more time with Dieter in his renovated townhouse, and to avoid this way a possible confrontation between him and her friends, they spent more time at her house than at his. He loved her better in a context of poverty. While she was moving among the down-and-out, he lavished her with attentions. He let her use his car any time; he bought her clothes and dinner out; he put up bookshelves, curtains, lightbulbs in her apartment; he pampered and praised her, making her feel that she was an illuminating presence in a chaotic universe. She slipped in and out of a kind of slangy street talk that she identified with blackness. He liked it. She told him the secrets she had learned about life lived on the margins, and about the effects of segregation on the imagination. She never, though, told him about the lie she was living, or how her liberation was won by it. She was terrified of his finding out, and in her longing to stay with him for years and years, she imagined leaving Boston with him, and that way leaving the lie behind, buried and gone.

There was a late spring snow that made May blossoms all the more profuse that year. Along Commonwealth Avenue the magnolia and dogwood spread handfuls of pinks and whites; cherry and appleblossom puffed along the sidewalks of Boston and Cambridge. G bolted from job to job, and imagined each one was a rung on an invisible ladder, which climbed through the fluffy trees to a point where there was a vista displayed. That vista was really a map of the world. Many of her friends now were Freedom Riders, heading south to join the Movement. Wanting to follow, but held back by a dread of her own secret exposing her, she worked all the harder at bringing cases against slumlords in Boston.

Her parents wondered what had happened to their brilliant daughter, the one who graduated early, Summa, who should have been, as they saw it, married at best, and a law student or writer at the very least. But the mother lived almost always in Italy now, and could forget from there, and the father had learned to turn his tolerance for disappointment into verse. The world was, daily, confirming the worst. He liked that. Neither parent nor lover knew how she was straining to rise to the top of that ladder and to see her way free.

Dieter continued to be fascinated by her friendships, espe-cially those with Africans, West Indians and Afro-Americans. As she breezed back and forth across boundaries usually im-passable for whites, he marveled at her character which gave her such access. At the same time her unwillingness to let him follow her there, and to let him share in these friendships, troubled him.

I think your attraction to those people must have a sexual basis, he teased her. You can't convince me otherwise, so don't try! I bet you feel that white men have failed you, or you did until we got back together, and so you moved in the direction of black men. Don't worry. I'm not mad, not jeal-ous, but I know I'm right.

You're not right, you're wrong, she said, reddening with the confusion that his argument produced in her. "Those people" are my friends, my best friends, and nothing else.

Well, why do you hide me away then?

You *are* jealous, she said with a delighted smile.

No. It's my fault for leaving you before. You were alone for too long—I mean, for a hot-blooded girl like you.

I didn't have any affairs, she insisted. I swear!

Well, you moved out of your house. You basically changed class, and you seem to want to change races. Where do I fit in?

You know where, she said, climbing onto his comfortable knees.

I still say—

Well, don't—

And both of their expressions glazed over, as eyes do when their owner decides to dream instead of see.

My bed's window looks into the cosmos, and offers as many optical delights as Mount Palomar with its relay satellite and dish antenna.
Comedy is the ceiling of society's self-understanding.

All those speeding galaxies are like sperm heading for the black hole, or The Womb of Being, and if you want my opinion, this similarity should lead a scientist to a profound truth. But my brother finally committed the ultimate sin when he stepped on the moon before me, a woman. Meantime I was mounting that percent of the air I could see, with my eyes floating between galaxies, quasars and even around the old big bang that set the universe in motion.
I don't believe in dying, and you might say I'm a modern spiritualist even where I stare out at a flat blue roof of snow.

Love, which excitedly insists that one individual is an exception to all the others, can be exhausted by this very excitement. Dieter drank too much, and so G did too, and every time they were together, they became drunk, and consequently they suffered the following day. Dieter dealt with the suffering by working all the more intensely on his book, locked up in his home with six-packs of beer, while G, who couldn't afford the cure of alcohol, became tremulous, fearful and subject to those harsh waves of anxiety that once lifted her up and over like efforts on the part of pure spirit, locked into substance, efforts actually liberating in intention.

It was late fall when Dieter's book was nearly complete that he got in the mood for change, again. He felt stultified by Boston and figured he should move to New York to ensure the success of his manuscript. He was not happy with himself, or the habits that had sustained him over those months. And he decided to switch from cigarettes to a pipe, from scotch to wine, and from his relationship to G to some X, Y, or Z who would not be time-consuming. He set a date, February first, for the delivery of his manuscript and himself.

Meanwhile he feared telling G of his new program. He didn't want her to suffer and tried, frantically, to think up a way of leaving her which would make her believe that she had brought it on herself. He lavished her with the lovingkindness of one who is leaving. He pitied her for not knowing what was coming. He dropped hints of his restlessness, and of his obsession with success.

> Before I'm forty I want to have an international reputation, he announced. I don't know if I can get that, starting from Boston.

She agreed that this might be a problem.

Everyone but G suspected Dieter of planning to depart. Augustine, among others, felt that Dieter was unable to commit himself to her because of her racial background. Others felt, on those rare occasions when they ran into him in the hall or her apartment, that he was a man who feared black men, that he was a hawk in dove's clothing. While he was jovial and courteous, fear danced in the sparkle of his eyes. During one encounter on the dark stairs, he and Augustine agreed to meet on their own; each one wanted to scrutinize the intentions of the other in relation to G.

It's essential to stay right up next to God. A disembodied ego, though, can experience nothing of the material world and may go mad, requiring the kind of investigation applied by scientists to their experiments.

However, complete objectivity, when applied to another person, is completely impossible. Empathy affects the information.

Law: a weak people cannot become strong and still remain committed to the ideology of weakness.

Either you are on the side of the rich or of the poor, and each condition, like a choice, is calling you deep into history.

Making symbols out of particulars is the job of terrorists, who express contemporary despair more concretely than almost anyone.

How to safeguard the object of your love in a world that holds no object more valuable than the material body—this is the impossible trick that the terrorist blows apart.

A light snow was falling outside. Inside a vent blasted a faint smell of fish onto Dieter's face, his hair blew back as if he was on board ship. Smoke rose to the ceiling and hung there while he and Augustine sipped on beers.

Are you bothered by Gemma's background? Augustine asked after a while.

Why would I be? You couldn't get much better, said Dieter with a conspiratorial smile. Blue blood is supposed to be the clearest in this country.

Blue blood? Augustine asked, curious. I never heard that expression.

I can't believe you lived in Boston this long, and haven't heard it.

Ah well. You know this city is as bad as the Deep South in many ways. . . . I never met her father, but Gemma's mother must have left because it was intolerable here.

I suppose *he* was intolerable. He's pompous, said Dieter.

And racist too?

I don't know about that. I think he's a moderate conservative type.

Well, he'd have to be somewhat liberal to marry her in the first place, Augustine noted. That's very rare. Interracial marriage occurred in Europe during the last war, I heard, but not here, on home ground.

What are you talking about? Dieter asked, straightening, and his bright eyes sparked as if viewing a far horizon across the sea. Who had an interracial marriage?

Gemma's parents, of course. That's what we're talking about.

Dieter's was a quick mind, and his thoughts now raced up and down every possible avenue, before finding the one that gave him the widest access. He shrugged and smiled.

Sorry, Augustine, he said, I was just drifting, getting distracted. Please go on with what you were saying. I agree that interracial marriage was rare here, is.

Yes. And that's the question: does her race bother you?

Live and let live. You know that's my attitude.

I know, but I mean would you be able to marry someone black, like Gemma?

I wouldn't marry anyone at this point in my life, man, he replied. Not even a rich white girl with a brain.

Augustine scrutinized Dieter carefully, seeing how deftly he was avoiding a direct response to his question. The avoidance in this case was the response he expected, but something more was troubling too. He waited for Dieter this time to speak.

Does Gemma talk to you about her family background? Dieter asked.

Sometimes. But really not much.

How would you describe her racial type?

Well, mulatto, I guess. And you?

I don't know the word for it, I guess.

Now they both stared off into a distant space and forgot each other and the necessity for conversation. Dieter knew at that moment he could utterly humiliate G by giving away her lie. But he drew back because it was more strange than he ever could imagine.

The next evening he went directly to G's apartment, after completing his quota of work for the day. The twilight lay blue on the rocky streets, and from down there, the light in her window, coming through bamboo and chintz, looked as innocent as a child's hair. Dieter went through the usual moves of opening drinks and smokes before confronting her directly with the knowledge he now had.

What do you think you're doing? he asked, his voice all outrage. You aren't any more black than I am!
I can't explain it.

I've met your brother, I've seen pictures of your parents. I even met your father. I know what you are.
She was frightened and her legs trembled. She sat on the edge of her bed, afraid that he would strike, or, worse yet, leave. She found she had no words of defense or explanation. It was like a dream of teeth falling out. No hard little words pressed over her tongue, her lips.

I could have told Augustine, then and there. I should have. He should know. I'm really shocked at you—overwhelmed. I always thought of you as completely honest.
He moved, paced and pointed, stressing her deception's effect on his trust. And his trust's importance in a love relationship. He wondered how she got away with it for so long, how she felt while she was getting away with it, and how she felt about herself.

She couldn't speak. Mute, she sat with her hands clenched on her lap, in a sweater, skirt and long socks, like a schoolgirl. He paused and looked at her as if seeing her anew. (Under this gaze she felt her color drawn off, as if by some vacuum that traveled through him to the stars.) In his eyes her skin tone and kinky hair took on a new appearance because of her lie. She was not, as it turned out, what she said she was to anyone but him, not black or white, but a mystery, which rhymed with history. Down the hall came the sounds of a Miles Davis melody, played over and over by one of her friends. She sat attentive and her eyes were fixed on the dark window. He moved over and stood near, where he imagined her as he had before, sexually tied to the men in the building, but now it was explicit in his thoughts. Still accusing her verbally he fell, then, onto her, and while she believed that he was making love to her, in his mind he was raping her.

When you take my place, the area around remains irrevocably vacant, even as I pass through it to get to the others who have left.

I miss a familiar voice is the truth, the salt of human sweat.

No one would give me credit for kindness every day that I resisted expressing my rage.

Perpetual dinner smells and lowered postures where I live. Nothing gained, but d--d and G-d, with gone blowing through. My hidden groom, out of a hand of five wishes, look at me now, too late to change.

Rain's on the river, ducks land on that waste, the sky is dense and low, blackbirds yell Let's go, let's turn off the sun and find our true colors.

I'm tired. Pull me, will you?

In the little fold of a child's arm I taste the world from a distance. Where I don't actually stand, my spirit is sucked out a drafty porthole—rain, snow, You, rain.

It was clear to everyone who knew her that, when Dieter left her, G was effectively destroyed. That she came from some privileged and educated background, black or white, was obvious to her friends, but it was now irrelevant in the face of her excessive drinking and her attraction to anonymity to the point of annihilation. She scraped bits of money together, just managing to pay her rent and eat meager food and drink chemically infected wines. She became and remained pale. Friends watched over her by taking advantage of her weakness in a way designed, also, to keep her from harm. Someone was always staying with her; someone always needed a place to stay. And that person then made sure that he or she and G had something to eat, that electric and fuel bills were paid, that the machines kept functioning for their survival.

In the following summer, Augustine left to return to South Africa and then to move to Geneva and his fiancee, permanently. Before his departure, he and others agreed that G was not black at all. They wondered if she had ties to the CIA, if she had, for all that time, been spying on them. It was not so much her lie that made them suspicious as her tie to Dieter, who seemed, in retrospect and with growing success in New York, to be suspect. Augustine left without saying any of this to G, and her other friends left too, heading south, or to New York, away from Boston, which they said was hell for any person of color, and none of them said anything to her either. It was a way of forgetting her.

G's apartment windows stayed open night and day to let the hot air circle around the room. Some changes occurred in the neighborhood and young whites moved in and became her friends. At all hours were the classic sounds of breaking glass, raised voices, music and cars. Assassination mushroomed, its cloud like a male organ disseminating smoke, and folk songs suggested that America's innocence lay before Columbus. Some of the white people in the building headed west, and told G to join them in Utah where they were going underground to manufacture weapons. After they left G was usually found seated on the stoop with a drink, a cigarette and an eager, questing expression that called people over to talk about things like student riots, the Kennedys and God.

It was months before any member of her family came near her.

However, one day A came looking for G. Perfumed and neatly coiffed, she rapped on the door of G's studio, then stood, with her nostrils compressed against the smells she associated with illness and poverty. She gave no indication that she was suffering from nervous cramps, a violent headache, symptoms of dread. The night before she dreamed she had won the Nobel Prize for Despair. Music fell down the stairs like a slinky going bang, zip, bang, all the way to her feet. When G opened the door, it was four on a rainy afternoon.

Why, said G instead of Hi.

To see you. If you're all right.

See? I am.

Can't I come in?

Sure.

A entered, tentatively. The single room contained a single bed, a table, two chairs, bookshelves containing books and clothes, a radio, a couch covered with sheets and pillows, and a wine bottle with a dripped-out candle stuck inside it.

A sat and then stood at the window, facing out at the rain.

Now. If you can tell me, she said to her daughter, someone or something that you want, I will get it for you. Or we will know, at least, what it is that you really want. Can you think of something?

G thought about Dieter intensely for several minutes, and then she thought of alcohol. Both were things she wanted. But she joined her mother at the window looking out.

I don't know, Mother. Outside there is a whole world, and I can't think of something I really want.

That means you're depressed, said A with finality.

It could mean I'm happy.

I wish I believed that but I don't. No, if you don't come with me, which you should, to Italy, then I think you should enter a hospital and get some treatment. Before you do something permanently harmful. I really do.

G was rocked by a violent shudder at the words *hospital* and *treatment*. It traveled the length of her spine, just as if she had one hand in water and one in light.

What's wrong? asked her mother.

A chill, she replied.

The rain clattered on the glass, cutting into the dust, forming runny lines.

Well, no wonder. Living here, you must be sick all the time. . . . Please listen to me. I want you to get well, to be happy. Come with me—or—if you could just see a psychiatrist—for this depression, whatever has brought you here.

I'll think about it, said G obediently.

I'll call to find out what you decide, said her mother.

All right, do, was G's passive response.

Gemma, her mother said, do you think a mentally ill person should be held responsible for their crimes? Are you capable of crime? Are you mentally ill? My uncle Joe was, of course, and my mother was, too. Do you think you inherited something? Or are you making decisions?

G gave her mother a radiant smile and opened her empty hands.

Mother, that's the question of my generation. Someone else will have to answer it.

Then A left and G watched her from her window as she exited the building, briskly, and hurried to her car with the pretense of ease and even pleasure built into the snap of her heels. It was August, 1963, and the March on Washington was no longer in progress. The rain in Boston fell as scattered showers.

If I see through myself, what am I seeing through?
When my sight goes way out, I don't hate anything. Even
when the rain never came. When it finally did, I lost laughs
under umbrellas of greens and little lambs stood woolly in the
wuthering storm, pages from THIS WONDERFUL WORLD
fluttering up pinafores and ribbons and the wind in them all.

I was so glad to be a child again, I slipped out of the glass
where my treasured dreams were all the more precious for the
night in which they were stored. And the tiny limbs on which
those raindrops spattered beat off the lie that there could be a
greater love than this—the love for *what is*.

I remember a desert where the sun fills my cells and I can rake
in the sand and this way begin a glassmaking effort.
You see, I let many facts fail and also their names and stood,
three fingers up, with my pulse buried in cloth.
I saw Saint Joan holding in her arms a little fruit and the
words, It's here—Charity!
The rain cleaned the glass until I stained where it had, and
now there was nothing but fiery light which also made a stain I
couldn't polish by hand.

I covered my face and didn't peek and this way kept hope safe
in the way of all concealed mercies. And when daylight again
illuminated my stains I rubbed the glass between the Testa-
ments with a cloth and fists.

Divinity flamed the sand from which this stained glass came.

That night G lay in the semi-darkness on her bed, her knees folded up to her belly, her eyes open. The raining was done and water alone dripped from the gutters. The occasional car greased by with a splashing sound. There was a party somewhere in the building (those who had not gone to Utah to build bombs were having fun) and G was alone in her place, preferring for this time to hear the music from a distance and to drink alone.

She remembered the school she had burned a hole in, a matter of miles away, and saw herself in the same hospital room T had once occupied, with the same nurse and fears. As if nothing had changed, she remembered her brother as a boy saying, I'll give you a reward if you do me a favor. And the reward and favor were just the same: that she should lean down and kiss, first his feet and then his stiff white organ in the woods where they lay. He laughed at her for her humiliation, he called her his little slave, since he was the master's son. And he said there was no such virtue as shame.

Now you can't start over, she said to herself. Her own shadow she envisioned as a little hunched figure, growing larger and larger, a proportion on a wall. The end.

She woke up as a child in a patch of warm sunshine, soaked by it, and realized at once her brother had abandoned her. She got up, brushed the sand off her face and pajamas, collected a deep breath of air, and looked for a path to the house they were visiting. A part of her still slept as she walked barefoot along the sand, looking into the hobbled spruce forest. Her mouth was a black O through which she breathed short quick gasps. She turned circles, seeking help which wasn't there. Active shadows flicked at the edges of the sand. Now she came to the end of the beach where stones were piled, and she walked back again, scanning the woods. The look of the lost: the pupils grow small, the eyelids hooded. She walked this way and that, but never fully awoke.

There was after all no path but flames of sand weaving between shrubs. She turned around three times and felt as if she were hanging by a thin thread from the round sun overhead, and was twirling in an immense and rejecting system. She tried to be confident and sang a little song, but it was fragile in the wake of the tidal sounds. She gulped and sat down, whimpering, and made an oval basin in the sand, where she could curl up under the sun. There she lay, glinting at sand, for one hour, two, three, while the tide rolled up close to the rim of her basin. And finally at nearly noon, she heard her name. There, way inside the woods she saw a dark-skinned woman with a well-known smile, carrying a bucket and shovel, calling her name.

Then she was thrown forward in her bed, as if knocked from behind and under, and tossed into a wholly new place. It was that kind of shock, but a speeded-up attack of despair, too, a lash of physical horror shot from inside. She threw herself forward, upright. I have to wake up. The hour was only around ten. She got up and stuffed her whiskey in her purse with the little money she had, plus toothbrush, comb and a change of underwear. I've got to wake up. She was shaking up and down.

G rushed through the damp warm summer night to Back Bay Station. There she wrote out a check, which would bounce, for a ticket to Ogden, Utah. The last train to New York left near midnight, and she took it. She was dressed in beatnik black and a pair of leather sandals molded to the shape of her feet. From New York she went on to Chicago, where she arrived the next day with $4.35, some of which she spent on a half pint of cheap scotch.

Next she took the train out of Chicago, west again, seated in the dome car through hours and hours of flat land, of lonely houses shooting out light in the night, until she stepped into the streets of Ogden, Utah, wide awake.

The air was as sweet as lake water. Relaxing wholly, she let herself be carried forward, step by step. Jupiter was the morning star. East by south she walked with the thick sky lifting light from under its rim, as if the sun was its secret and clouds were playing in it.

With no more money and no more alcohol, in a dry state she washed herself in the air, gave herself a new name and aim and disappeared.